The Stolen Crate

HELEN SHACKLADY

Published in 2002 by Onlywomen Press, Limited, London, UK.

With financial support from London Arts.　**⋮ ⋰ LONDON**
⋰ ⋅ ARTS

ISBN 0-906500-72-9

British Library Cataloguing-in-Publication Data.
A Catalogue record for this book is available from the British Library.

Typeset by Chris Fayers, Cardigan, Wales.
Printed and bound in Great Britain by Mackays of Chatham Limited.

For Jane

1

"For God's sake, woman," Liz crashed through from the back kitchen, "stop now! You're driving me mad!" She was wiping her hands on what looked like an oily rag, but which I soon recognised as one of my tee shirts.

"What?" I lifted my bow and assumed what I hoped was a butter wouldn't melt demeanour. I wouldn't mention the shirt.

"You know. You're doing this on purpose to wind me up." She threw the shirt at my feet.

"But I have to practise this," I said reasonably, "I'm recording tomorrow with that country and western singer."

She was right all the same. Playing the instrumental break from 'A soft place to fall' over and over again was my not so subtle way of getting back at her for bringing pieces of her motorbike into the house, spreading them on the kitchen floor, and then putting selected items on the table in the dining area, where she could fiddle with them, droning contentedly to herself.

"Anyway," I changed tack and put my violin and bow carefully in their case, "don't worry, darling, I'm stopping now. I've got to go and see Toni." Ha, one up to me. I wasn't going to ask her to accompany me on a visit to my old friend.

"You're not going out." She strode around me, blocking the door into the hall, "You're staying here."

"What?" The beginnings of genuine anger frayed at the edges of my act, "You can't say that."

"I just have. You're staying here to help me tidy up this . . . this tip."

Somewhere she was right again, the place was a mess. Piles of music, instruments and photographic equipment

5

jostled for space, a half unpacked box of books lay on the settee, the fireplace was full of ash and the whole room was liberally strewn with coats, scarves, shoes and odd socks. Still, I wasn't going to let her bully me like this.

"Don't be so ridiculous, how are you going to stop me? By force?" Even I was suprised at how annoyed I sounded.

"Don't push me, I'm stronger than you."

We glared at each other, the dangerous moment teetering on a knife edge.

"Well, I'm fatter than you," I said without thinking. The wave of anger between us receded abruptly, and I saw the telltale softening in her dark eyes.

"So, what do you plan to do? Sort of bounce over me and roll out of the door?" Her voice was gentle.

My own mouth quivered, "Something like that."

She smiled, and curled her hand slowly towards me, tracing the outline of my ear with one slim finger, "Let's give it a try, then."

I swayed, and surrendered to the enchanting inevitable.

Afterwards, though, I lay in our bed looking at her face pillowed, eyes shut, on my shoulder, and wondered where we were going. I had been in ecstasy last autumn when, in the first heady flush of overwhelming attraction and emotional overload, she had suggested that she should move permanently from Somerset to the north to be with me, and even more enraptured when we quickly decided to rent a house together, my own flat being far too tiny even for a couple without a propensity for ferocious arguments and blissful makings up. In this unwelcome instant of sadness, with Liz apparently lost to me in sleep, I asked myself if it had been a mistake. If I had a type, she wasn't it. It didn't help that I'd known from the beginning that she was moody, oddly secretive and deeply amoral, had had more lovers than I could bear to imagine and had never lasted even a year in a relationship. She had the uncanny gift of arousing in me a dreadful fury I never knew I possessed, and we'd had some horrible wounding rows, which, unused to such naked emotion, I loathed completely. And yet. . . Her even breathing flowed through me in a soothing swell, dissipating my uncharacteristic bleakness. I knew she cared for me in her way. She had put a stop to some of my bad habits, like

6

consuming large amounts of vodka and then smoking in bed, she didn't drink as much as me, she rarely smoked and hardly ever touched drugs. She was a wonderful cook, and would ply me with all sorts of tasty concoctions, nagging me to eat properly, and she never seriously complained about my erratic schedule. As far as I knew, and I had my spies, her intense passions hadn't led yet to her being unfaithful when I was away with the band, which was my worst dread, she made me laugh like a drain, and she made an effort to get on with my friends. I studied the way her recently cut almost black hair stuck up from her forehead, her smooth untroubled features and the irresistable curve of her mouth in repose, and felt the still unbelievable sweetness of her body and long legs wrapped around me. I had come full circle. Oh dear, I thought, I'm crazy about you.

She stirred, and her eyelids flickered, "You're looking at me."

"So I am." I slid down a few inches, and we rearranged ourselves so that our noses touched. "Fancy a cup of tea?" I asked. We kissed idly.

"Mm, in a minute." Her hands moved, "Do you really have to go to Toni's?" We kissed less idly.

"Nah." There was a particular reason why I wanted to see Toni today, but it had slipped my mind.

"Good."

A spiteful wind hurled bullet sprays of rain against the window, the quilts sighed and settled around us, and the silky shifting of muscle beneath her warm skin drove conscious thought away. After all, I didn't know of a better way to spend a foul Sunday afternoon in February.

"Oh my," she lay back on the pillows, "I really need that cup of tea now."

"Help." Flopped on top of her, I spoke into her neck, "I think my skeleton's gone missing."

"You just don't know when to stop."

"Excuse me, this was your idea. . ."

A thunderous knocking at the front door interrupted our snickering sweet nothings.

"Hell," she rolled out from under me, "I'll get rid of whoever it is, then we can stay here for ever."

7

I managed to move enough to switch on the bedside lamp and see raindrops on the window pane turn into running diamond sparkles in the light. Giving little groans and stretches, I watched her delicious shape as she pulled on her shirt and sweater, opened the window and leaned out.

"Ag!" she said, a bit rudely, "what do you want?"

I pulled up the quilt against the cold blast of air.

"I want to come in. It's fucking 'orrible out here."

All our neighbours would hear her cross voice.

"Well, the door's open. Down in a minute." She shut the window, picked up her jeans from the floor and grimaced at me, "I'll put the kettle on. So much for that, sweetie."

Actually, I wasn't too surprised. During the few weeks Liz and I had shared my flat on the top floor of her parents, Pat and Tom's, house, Ag had complained incessantly about the noise we made, but once we had moved out, she had taken to popping round at odd times to eat our biscuits and moan about the unendurable nature of her seventeen year old life. All the years I had lived in the flat, I never thought that she liked me much, yet I was coming to the realisation that Liz and I had been elevated to the status of some kind of honorary aunts, who could be trusted not to relay the gorier details of what she and her friends got up to. I tested my strength by gradually getting out of bed, scratted around for some clothes, and followed Liz downstairs.

"How d'you do that?"

"Sorry?" I looked up from shovelling coal on the fire to see Ag's undeniably lovely face scowling at me.

"Make a fire so quickly. Mum and Dad spend hours pratting around with ours, and it always goes out."

"Um. . . Chloe taught me, it was one of her talents." This was true, we had always joked that my ex, Chloe, could light a fire with a bucketful of water and a spent match. Still whoozy, I lit a cigarette and let myself sink into a little reverie about all the things I did a certain way because that was the way Chloe had done them. Eating the pips in apples, always walking on one particular side of some of the streets in town, never throwing bits of dropped food on the fire, even orange peel. . . Would I stay the same, or would I pick up a whole load of Liz's idiosyncracies?

"Kate!" They were both shouting at me, and Liz plonked a mug of tea on the floor in front of my knees.

"Come back from wherever you are, earthling," her eyes crinkled and my heart somersaulted, "Ag wants us to sign her petition."

I sucked gratefully at my tea, "What petition?"

"Jesus, did you hear a word I was saying?" Ag rolled her eyes, "Against the Bradley development."

"Oh yes, I've heard of that." I had too. The controversy over this proposed state of the art shopping centre on a greenfield site near a depressed little town a few miles north of the city had spilled for months from the letters page of our local newspapers into the sections usually reserved for WI reports and obituaries of local worthies. "I thought they'd got planning permission anyway," I added, to prove I had a toehold in reality.

"Bribery and corruption," Ag thumped the settee, releasing a cloud of dust, "we're demanding a proper enquiry, and," she lowered her voice, "some of us are planning direct action."

"God, tunnels and that?"

I was quite impressed, it was nice to see that Ag had an outside interest. If I'd known where all this would lead, though, I might not have been so sanguine.

"Maybe. Sign here." She shoved a chewed biro and a photocopied sheet, headed by BAG! (Bradley Action Group), in front of me, and I made my mark under Liz's bold flourish.

"Ta." She settled back, "Oooh, Liz, did I tell you about Mark and that hairdressing tutor?" She started on some scurrilous tale about people at her college, where Liz had somehow wangled her way into teaching evening photography classes, and I let my mind wander again. The room might be spectacularly untidy, but it was very cosy with the fire crackling, the dark safely outside and Liz's giggling exclamations punctuating Ag's narrative.

"Shit!" Their voices stopped like a switched off soundtrack at my uncouth exclamation. I'd remembered why I wanted to go to Toni's today. "Issy," I said to their open mouths, "Issy was coming down today. That's why I was meant to see Toni, Issy's there."

"Who's Issy?" The faintest glimmer of suspicion hovered in Liz's question.

"You know, Toni's friend. I told you all about her, she moved up to Kirktown a few years ago when she split up with her girlfriend." Every now and then, I tried to give Liz a history lesson on all the permutations and scandal which formed the background to the social scene in the city, but I was never sure how much she absorbed, and I felt I couldn't present her with a written test to check she was safe to let out into the pubs and clubs without saying the wrong thing to the wrong person.

"Ah. Why do you want to see her anyway?" Her hands had gone still, and Ag stiffened like a deer hearing twigs snapping in the distance.

"It was just about music. She's getting some street band together, and wanted me to look at some tunes with her. . ."

She'd phoned a couple of weeks ago, and I'd completely forgotten. So much for the huge calendar which Liz had stuck on the kitchen wall, and on which I was meant to write all my commitments and the dates when I'd be away.

"Well," Liz had relaxed, "ring Toni now, and see if she's still there. If you go in the car, it'll only take you a few minutes to pop round."

I was amazed. The clapped out Fiesta, our first and only major joint purchase, was normally our favourite bone of contention.

"I'm going anyway," Ag got to her feet, "things to do, people to meet." She left, as noisily as she had arrived.

"Phone." Liz put her hand on my shoulder, then wandered back towards the kitchen. I moved a stack of bills, retrieved my address book from under a chair, and pressed the numbers.

"Toni? I'm really sorry, I got held up," I gabbled, "is Issy still there?" I listened to her calm tones at the other end, and shouted through to where I assumed Liz was, "Liz? Issy's staying for supper, do we want to go as well?"

"Not me, I've got calls to make." There was a clang of metal, "Ow. . . hang on a tick. . ."

"Just a minute," I said to the patient receiver and waited until Liz reappeared, a lump of greasy iron in her hand.

"If you come back," her face gave nothing away, "I'll cook

something for us. Green rice?"

Wow. "No, thanks anyway," I smiled down the line, "Liz has got culinary plans. But I'll come round for a bit now, if that's ok."

I put the phone down, ran upstairs for a quick shower and found some slightly more respectable clothes. Green rice was the ultimate, cooked to a recipe Liz would never divulge to me. "If I tell you, you'll only go and try and do it yourself, and it'll be a waste of ingredients. Anyway, it's a knack which only comes with practice." She could be like a home economics teacher sometimes, "You stick to washing up, dear."

Still a bit damp, I went downstairs to stand between the sitting room and dining area. Liz was sitting bent over the table, studying its engine studded surface as if it was a chess puzzle.

"I'll be off, then," I said. " See you in an hour or so."

"Yeah," she didn't look up, "have a nice time."

"Thanks."

She lifted her head, and flashed her quick smile at me. Suddenly awkward, I moved forward to hug the strong brace of her shoulders.

"I'm sorry," I found myself saying.

"I know," she rubbed her head against me, "I'm a real pain sometimes. I'll clear this away."

"And I'll do some tidying up, I promise."

"Don't forget these," she reached out and fished the car keys from a cluttered bowl at the back of the table, "love you, Kate."

I took the keys and hugged her tighter, "Oh Liz. . ."

"Get along with your bother."

My happiness complete, I skipped out to the car and drove to Toni's.

I was looking forward to an hour or so of stimulating conversation about love and music, two of my most treasured subjects. I'd met Toni through Chloe, since they both worked at the university, and at first had been totally in awe of her. She was relatively high up in the English department, and reminded me of the scary headmistress of my secondary school, giving the impression of being frightfully intellectual and super organised. She knew absolutely everyone, had her finger on everything that was going on, and was extremely difficult to lie to, which was inconvenient.

When it had gone pear-shaped between Chloe and me, however, and especially when Chloe had left the city, she had revealed herself to be a kind hearted softie, and had given up hours to listen to my weeping and wailing. I had also been reassured to discover that she was nearly as untidy at home as I was. She had performed the same ministering angel role to her best friend, Issy, when Issy's great love affair with Bel had later come to its famously cataclysmic end. I tried to meet up with Toni at least once a month, so I could catch up on who was sleeping with who, and other important information I needed to keep abreast of current affairs. I hadn't seen that much of Issy, a fine trumpet player, since her abrupt move to take over a music shop in Kirktown, way up north across the bay.

"Well, Kate," Issy pulled a face at me, "I don't need to ask how it's going. You look disgusting."

We were sitting, surrounded by heavy looking books and stacks of files, drinking more tea. There were streaks of grey in Issy's wavy brown hair, and the lines on her intelligent face had deepened. Her eyes still held that slightly frozen look which had hung there since Bel had left.

"Oh, I don't know," I demurred, "it's not all plain sailing . . ."

"What's she like? Tell me everything."

"Um . . . tall." I couldn't think how to describe Liz, and I knew I was blushing. When it came down to it, it was much harder to talk about myself than rabbit on about other people.

"Come on," Toni was beginning to laugh, "she's absolutely gorgeous, Iss, and unbelievably sexy . . ."

"Tell me about the band." I tried to divert them.

"Shut up. How did you meet? When did you get together?" Issy wouldn't give in.

"Oh God, you've heard me talk about my friend Emily in Somerset? Liz was her neighbour, and that's where I met her. Then we sort of ended up in France together . . ."

"When you rescued Chloe from those nutters she got involved with," Toni nudged Issy, "I told you about it."

"I want to hear for myself. How come Liz was involved?"

12

I sighed, "It's a complicated story. Liz had her own reasons for wanting to find the nutters." They may have been my friends, but there was no way I wanted to explain how Liz's shady dealings had led us both to France and to our unlikely affair.

"You're hopeless," Issy was laughing as well, "can't you find one for me, though?"

"God, one of her's enough. Are you still. . .?"

"Yeah, single. I think I've given up actually. I'm devoting my life to being a respectable pillar in the Kirktown community, making a noise in the Chamber of Trade, going to local history classes, getting this band off the ground for the Charter parade. . ."

"The what?" I had succeeded in getting her off on another track.

"The Charter parade. This year," she adopted a school marm tone, "you'll be interested to hear, is the 750th anniversary of the granting of Kirktown's market charter, which was a milestone in the town's history. I hope you're taking notes. Anyway, there's going to be a big parade in July, and historical enactments and stuff like that. So," she suddenly looked animated and more like the old Issy, "I've got together with this percussion chappie, and we're putting together a street band, a bit like. . ."

"Mill Street Dykes Deluxe!" I remembered the name of the samba band Issy used to play in.

"Yeah, but if we restricted it to dykes in Kirktown, there'd be me and a retired librarian. We've got enough people interested, and I've got some nice tunes but," she looked uncertain, "I think I need some help with arranging them to give parts to the instruments we've got. So I thought of you, since you're the big cheese in the music world now."

"Aw, get lost. I'm not sure, but I'll have a go. . .have you got them here?"

"Yeah, but," she hesitated again, "really it would be better if you could come up to the shop, and we can tootle on some instruments together, hear how they sound. You can play the saxophone a bit, can't you? How about one afternoon this week? I need to get this sorted quickly."

"Er, um, I'm a bit busy. . ." I tried to visualise the kitchen calendar.

"You'll get paid. We've been promised loads of money from a local firm, Boltons, they make that revolting health margarine. . ."

"I'll do it."

"You tart. OK, when?"

"Thursday afternoon?"

"Fine, you can get a train from here, if you want."

"Done." I turned back to Toni, "What else is new?"

"Not a lot," she looked vaguely sly, "I saw Rosie the other day. We're going to a concert together."

I ignored her expression, "That's nice, d'you like her?"

"You old hypocrite. It wasn't me who had to stop in mid-flow and jump over her garden wall to escape from her girlfriend."

"It was nothing like that. Anyway," I became smug, "that's all in the past now." My unsuccessful pursuit of the delightful Rosie had no doubt afforded endless amusement to the gossiping classes last summer. We clacked merrily on until I happened to glance at the clock, "Oh dear, I must go, Liz is cooking."

"Ooooh," they both chorused, "don't be late, she'll leave it to burn in the oven, she'll lock you out, she'll hit you with the frying pan."

"You're just jealous," I tossed my head, and, drove home, my angst quite forgotten.

2

"Did you ever sleep with her?" Liz, fresh from the bath, was towelling her hair, and her question was muffled.

"Sleep with who?" Back in bed, and full of green rice, I turned another page of my thriller, then peered up to see her drop the towels on to the floor. "Hey! Take those back into the bathroom, if we're being house proud."

"Blimey." She grumbled her way along the passage, and came back with the nail scissors.

"And don't cut your toenails straight on to the carpet. Use the wastepaper basket."

"I wish I'd never started this." She moved the bin from the corner then sat sulkily on the edge of the bed, facing away from me. After a few snips and mutters, however, she reached for my hand and put it on her naked back.

"This is so romantic," I remarked, when she had finished one foot and started concentrating on the other. Secretly, I blessed the fact that we had central heating, and I could feel all her movements from her bones outwards.

"Hm?" She threw the scissors in the general direction of a chest of drawers, "Am I losing my mystery then?" She clambered in next to me.

"You'll always be a mystery to me." I wasn't joking.

"That's the way I like it, keep 'em guessing."

"So I noticed. . .aren't you tired?"

She lifted her mouth from my throat, "Do you want me to stop?" The tenderness in her question pierced the guards around my heart.

"No, never," I breathed, and let myself fall into unmappable ecstasy.

"Well, did you?" she said later, twisting a finger through my curls.

"Did I what?"

"God, sleep with Issy."

Our bodged curtains didn't fit that well, and a passing car briefly illuminated her face. An odd shadow of vulnerability in her expression caught me by surprise. I pretended I hadn't seen it.

"No, I certainly did not!" I relented, "Well, we sort of thought about it once, but we were both too miserable, so we got very drunk instead."

Her shoulders started to heave.

"I know this is a difficult concept for you to grasp."

"Why were you too miserable? Hee hee."

"I was still upset over Chloe, and she was devastated about Bel leaving."

"Bel?" She gave a little jerk, "Not Bel Brown, bit shorter than me, heavier built, mousey-ish curly-ish hair, really nice eyes, very yummy?"

"Yes." The description was spot on.

I lifted my head, "You don't know her, do you?"

"I knew her years and years ago at college in London. We were great mates." Even in the dim light, I knew her face was wicked.

"You didn't! Is there anyone you haven't slept with?"

She laughed even more, "I think between us we pretty much covered all the bases. Well, I'll be darned, she went out with your friend Issy. How did she end up here? I wondered what had happened to her."

"I'm sure I've told you all this already. It was a massive scandal."

"Tell me again. I like your stories, they're nice and restful."

Why was I such a sucker for her? She entwined herself more comfortably around me, and I whispered out the terrible tale.

When I was with Chloe, we saw quite a bit, on and off, of Toni and Issy and their closest friends, Eleanor and Amy. Compared with me, they were at the slightly older and more respectable end of the scene. Toni was a lecturer, Issy gave brass lessons around the city schools, and Eleanor and Amy were both solicitors. We all tended to regard these two as the ideal couple, and a shining role model for everyone else who muddled along in relationships ranging from the precarious to the downright disastrous. They looked alike, although Eleanor was taller and thinner, they both had their hair cut in similar not too way out styles, they had a nice house, they both drove small not quite top of the range hatchbacks, and they devoted a lot of time, professional and private, to good causes. Of the four friends, Issy was probably the most disreputable, although this was too strong a word, with a tendency for short-lived affairs with wilder women. All this changed when Bel appeared. She was a gardener who came from no-one knew quite where, and after dallying around for a few months, one hot summer homed in on Issy like a guided missile. Issy was completely smitten. Within a month, Bel had moved into her house, and the two of them were giving supper parties and being lovey dovey in the nightspots. All this coincided with my split from Chloe, and, to my shame, I was far too wretched to be happy for Issy.

The affair imploded dramatically the following summer. Fractionally more compos mentis, I became aware, during the times I was in the city in between going away with the band, of some peculiar, ugly undercurrent beneath the apparently placid surface of these partnerships. Toni had a tendency to clam up whenever I asked how Eleanor and Amy or Issy and Bel were doing. I realised why one evening when I bumped into the four of them at the Anglers, a pub taken over by women, down by the canal. I sat at their table for an hour or so, until the weird disjointed vibe running through their superficially cheery conversation drove me away. A couple of weeks later, Toni caught me at home,

"Come round and help me. Issy's been here all week. She's kicked Bel out, and she's in a state."

I rushed over, for once more concerned for Issy than seeking hot gossip, and was thoroughly frightened by her grey face and icy composure.

"Well, Kate," she said through rigid lips, "it turns out that Bel and Amy have been sleeping together for the past month. I never want to see either of them again. I've been utterly betrayed."

To say I was stunned would be too trivial. At least Chloe and I had been years beyond the passionate honeymoon stage when we started being unfaithful to each other. Toni drew me to one side, "She won't eat anything except peach yoghurt, and then she throws it right up again."

For the next month, when I could, I helped Toni watch Issy like a hawk, both of us terrified that she might crack up completely. Bel hastily left the city; a distraught Eleanor and a repentant Amy tried to patch up their relationship; and the hapless Toni tried to be a friend to the couple and to Issy while keeping them apart.

"I can't help it, Kate, I love her," Eleanor had confided to me in tears one alcohol-fuelled evening when she'd turned up at my flat, "I want things back the way they were. I don't care if you think I'm mad. Anyway," this was a few drinks later, "she says it was only a fling and she doesn't know what came over her and she didn't enjoy it much, ha!"

In the end, Issy decided to move to Kirktown, but I don't think she had spoken much to Eleanor, and certainly never to Amy, since. The couple were still together, and I saw them occasionally, yet their lustre had definitely worn off, and in some obscure, irrational way, I had felt let down by them.

"I don't know why," I came to the end of my ramblings, "maybe it's just the feeling that they should have been above that kind of thing, especially when Amy was Issy's friend. And it was dreadful how. . .how broken Issy was, I'm not sure if she's even recovered yet. Liz? Liz?" The faintest suggestion of a snore told me she was fast asleep. I kissed her cheek, and shut my eyes.

During the next few days, I rashly concluded that my life was perfect. Liz and I seemed to have sailed into an unusually calm and affectionate patch, the recording session went well and I was promised more work, the band had a lucrative weekend on Tyneside ahead, and the weather cleared up. On Thursday lunchtime, I hopped on the local train to Kirktown, leaving Liz about to drive off and take some photographs of a country house for an estate agent, one of her little earners. We hadn't even argued over her using the car when I could have done with it. The train rattled along by the estuary, and I looked out of the window at the shimmering mudflats to see a swooping flock of birds flash like a living firework as low sunlight caught their intricately synchronised wheeling and turned them into a magical shoal of airborn fishes. Pure joy bubbled through me, and I let myself forget the tiny niggle at the back of my mind, brought on by what Liz had said the previous night.

It had been very late when I got in from our regular Wednesday session at the Folk Club, and by the time I had showered off the miasma of alcohol fumes and tobacco smoke, Liz had turned the light off, and was lying innocently with her eyes closed. I slipped in next to her, and nearly dozed off straight away.

"Darling. Darling Kate," she said huskily, which should have warned me, but I'd had a few, "you're away from Friday morning until Sunday afternoon, aren't you?"

"Mm." It was some Seabord festival on Tyneside, and we had a series of gigs lined up in different venues.

"Would you like me to come and pick you up on Sunday?" How nice she could be sometimes.

"Mm." I made the effort, "We should finish by two or three, I'll let you know where we'll be."

"It's just that I'm doing a little job for someone, so I probably won't be here on Friday night. It's nothing very exciting, but it's out of town."

"Fine, lovely, earn lots of money, 'night sweetie." I really was very tired, and in any case, I tried not to make a habit of prying too closely into her financial affairs.

"'Night, angel." Within a minute, I was dead to the world.

Now, of course, I wondered what on earth she was doing. Don't be paranoid, I told myself, you'd be able to tell if it was another woman, she never questions your going away with the band, it'll only be some boring photographs. I stomped determinedly on my worries, and put my mind to enjoying an afternoon with Issy. The little town bustled in the winter sunshine, and she seemed very much at home in her neat shop with its rows of secondhand CD's, shelves of music and stands of gleaming instruments. I just about know my way around a saxophone, and we had a very jolly time, drinking coffee from her machine and playing through parts on a selection of her stock. Her steady trickle of customers and people with CD's to sell or exchange didn't seem to mind our noise either, and I was tickled by how she appeared to know them all, and the way she nattered blithely while making what she later insisted were ruthless deals.

"You like it here, don't you?" I asked when we'd more or less finished writing down harmonies, and were sitting at the back of the shop, drinking yet more coffee.

She looked surprised, "Yes, I suppose I do. It's a funny place, but I'm getting quite fond of it."

"Don't you ever get bored, and feel the urge to come down for a night on the town?"

"Nah," she swirled the contents of her cup, "I'm settling for boredom over crisis any day. I manage to amuse myself."

The throaty roar of a motorbike in the alley behind the shop almost drowned her words. There were a few scrapes and bumps, then I heard solid footsteps moving along the alley and thumping up a hidden staircase. A series of crashes and creaks came from overhead.

"Jeanie," Issy said, an indulgent cast to her face, "I did the flat out above here, and she rents it. Mind you, the landlord doesn't know, he thinks I just use it for storage." So she hadn't changed too much.

The stairs suffered more punishment, the back door of the shop swung open, and in came Issy's tenant, rubbing grimy hands together,

"It's bloody freezing still. Hey Iss."

"Hey babe."

She was a sturdy young woman with very short fair hair, and her broad, snub-nosed face, even when pinched with cold, radiated youthful vigour. I suddenly felt very old.

"This is Kate," Issy flapped her hand, "Jeanie. She's a motorbike mechanic."

"Oh," I attempted not to sound like a maiden aunt, "my. . . um, Liz, has a motorbike."

"What kind?" She was giving me a merciless onceover.

"The kind that's in bits all over the kitchen floor."

She smiled. I was obviously not too far beyond the pale, "She should bring it to me. Amateur mechanics are the worst. I think I've seen you before."

I was thinking the same, "Must have been out in town somewhere."

"Yeah, probably." She knelt down, and started rummaging through a box of tapes on the floor.

"Don't steal all the good ones," Issy scolded, then turned back to me, "we're expecting the first cheque from Bolton's any day now, so I can send you some money when it arrives."

There was a snort from the box, "Make sure you get it soon. They're going to the wall."

"Rubbish!" Issy's response was instant, "Where d'you hear that?"

"Everyone knows. It's all over town. It's since they've been taken over by that American conglomerate." She pronounced the word with relish, "Asset stripping, innit. They'll close it down, put half the town out of work, no-one will be able to afford their bikes, and I'll have to go to London, where I'll probably end up homeless and on crack."

"Don't be daft, they're as safe as houses," Issy frowned at the broad back. "Don't listen to her, Kate, you'll get your dosh."

"Well, really, I haven't done much except have fun."

"I thought that was always your aim in life anyway," she grinned, "getting paid for getting drunk, scraping out a few tunes then falling over."

"You swine, I hardly ever do that now."

"I believe you."

"Iss," Jeanie's voice halted our inanities, "Can I borrow your van on Sunday?"

"No!" Again her reply was immediate. "Why? Where do you want to go?"

Jeanie's ears were pink, "Aw, come on, please. I want to take someone somewhere, and it's too cold for the bike."

"Is it some poor girl? What are you up to now? How long do you want it for?"

"Please, please, please, nice kind Issy. I'll pay for the petrol and I'll fix the door."

Issy sighed, "Well, all right, but make sure you bring it back by midnight. I don't want to be stuck without transport on Monday morning."

Jeanie jumped up, "Ah, thanks Issy. I'll take really good care of it, I promise, and I won't play with any rough children. I'll come by your place and pick it up on Sunday morning. Taraa for now." She beamed at us and backed out of the door, a pile of tapes held to her chest.

"And don't play those too loud until after the shop's shut!" Issy shouted after her.

I remembered where I'd seen her before, at a women's disco, snogging enthusiastically with some other young thing. I had opened my mouth to impart this information to Issy, when she spoke first,

"You might think I've gone really weird, but having her around is like. . .it's like having a teenage daughter all of a sudden. I feel I have to keep an eye on her and stuff."

I shut my mouth.

"Just don't sneak upstairs and read her diary," I said eventually, "that's the worst mother trick."

"I've been tempted to search her pockets for pills, isn't it awful, we must be getting old."

I giggled, "And this from a woman who did it in the dining room of the Anglers after that street band dinner."

She blushed. "It was after closing time, it wasn't as if people were still eating. And that waitress was divine, I just couldn't resist her."

Glad to see the old Issy almost back, I pressed on, "Where was she from?"

"Oh God, she was Dutch. Don't remind me. Anyway," she gave me a kick, "how did you know about it? You were on tour at the time."

"Get real, we all knew. I heard as soon as I came back."

We tittered and reminisced some more, then I caught the train back to get ready for the jaunt with the band.

My good mood continued, and I climbed into the band's van on Friday full of bonhomie. Liz had smothered me with kisses at the door, giving me a load of lovely nonsense about how my going away for two nights would make it all the more wonderful when I came back, and I was sappy enough to nip back upstairs and take one of her shirts to sleep in. I surveyed the band with benevolence, they were the best band in the world and I was lucky to be a part of it. Fred and Jo, solid and reliable, Bill, my friend, and even tetchy Dave. . .

"God, Kate, what're you on?" Bill gave me a curdled look, "You've got this nasty sickly smile on your face."

"It's lerve," I said unwisely, and yawned pointedly.

Dave frowned. Of all of them, he found it hardest to adjust his mindset to the possibility that I wasn't just experimenting until the right man came along. Still, he did his best.

"Liz not coming along at all this weekend?" he asked casually.

"She's popping across to pick me up on Sunday afternoon," I yawned smugly again.

"How nice. Just make sure you don't run off before you've helped us pack up."

I knew he didn't mind Liz turning up at gigs since she was an extra pair of capable hands to lift and carry, and her nearly automatic habit of snapping away at the band with her camera made him feel like a rock star. After about the worst possible beginning, she was gradually becoming accepted, which made life a lot easier, and somehow lessened the twinges of anxiety and dreariness which periodically assailed me when I was away. This weekend, however, looked set to be a happy one. We sang all the rude songs we knew on the way to Tyneside, then plunged into a whirl of setting up, playing our little hearts out, packing up and moving on to the next venue, interspersed with the usual intervals of arguing, eating unhealthy food and drinking. Fatigue and a smidgin of medicinal vodka ensured that I didn't miss Liz too much in my tacky bed and breakfast room, and I looked forward to her arrival on Sunday. I should have known that it was all too good to last.

The second I lifted my head as we reached the end of our set on Sunday afternoon and saw her leaning against the side wall of the hall, I knew something was terribly wrong. Her face was as stiff and her body as set as those of a stranger, and I felt instantly sick. I could sense my own cheekbones going solid, and it took all my self-control to smile nicely and bluff my way through an encore. She was there in a corner when we came backstage, and my heart gave a great leap before sinking into the icy waters of my stomach.

"Hi, sweetheart," she put her arms out, giving a forced half smile, and I let myself stand in her rigid embrace, some part of me already gauging from the feel of her body the depth of the crisis. My guts eased a fraction, and I gave her lips a neutral kiss. It was bad, but not terminally catastrophic.

"Hi, my love," I kept my voice even and pleasant, "Just got to clear up, then I'll be with you."

"Give you a hand," she mumbled, and released me. A few months ago, I would have demanded to know what was wrong right away, and probably burst into tears. Now I decided that experience was making me prematurely wise, and that I would sneakily bide my time until she cracked and spilled the beans herself. I didn't have to speak to her much while we helped the band to pack up, and once in the car, I pleaded exhaustion. After a few cheerful comments about the weekend, I shut my eyes and pretended to doze, letting her get on with her best impression of a volcano about to erupt after centuries of lulling nearby inhabitants into the mistaken belief that it is extinct.

Back at home, I switched on the hot water and central heating, made some tea and unpacked my bags, ignoring the monosyllabic grunts with which she answered my innocuous questions, and then ran myself a very deep and very hot bath. I immersed myself in a cumulus of bubbles and waited, my rational mind battling with the hideous lurking dread. It definitely wasn't another woman, if something had happened to my family, she would have told me right away, if she had decided to move. . .I stopped that line of thought, and concentrated on having a bet with myself on what her opening line would be. It was a toss up between, "You're not going to like this," and "You're not going to approve of this," and I had settled on the former when I heard her heavy tread on the stairs.

She glowered into the bathroom, and lowered herself on to the loo seat, her head in her hands.

"Kate," her voice was resigned, "I hesitate to say this, but I'm in a spot of bother."

3

I made myself wiggle my toes as if I was enjoying my soak, and told myself I was cross because I had lost my bet. "What sort of bother?"

"Oh God," she groaned and lifted her head, "it's to do with that little job I did on Friday."

"Oh." I scooped some more bubbles over me, and felt a bit better, "Did you break your best camera or something?"

She looked confused, then put her head back down, "No, no. . .it wasn't exactly that kind of job. It was a driving job."

I washed my ears. Maybe my hearing had been affected by years of listening to loud live music. "I'm sorry, what?"

"A driving job!" A brief shot of exasperation animated her, "I had to drive a van."

"A van?" I was beginning to sound like my granny years ago, when we had tried to explain to her what a cash machine was.

"Jesus, Kate! One of those big boxy things with four wheels."

At least she was coming back from that remote terrain where no-one else could tread.

She gathered speed, "I had to go to some god-forsaken spot in the borders on Friday afternoon, pick up a van, drive it down to Birmingham, load it up and drive it back. . ." she stopped when she saw my face.

"You went to Birmingham?" I squeaked.

"Well, it's not the fucking moon. Anyway. . ."

24

All the awful feelings I had never really experienced until I met her were fighting to come to the surface. I was very frightened, and could sense the despairing anger seeping into my voice, "It wasn't drugs again, was it?" I wasn't going to cry.

"No!" She almost stamped her foot, "Why do you always think the worst of me? It was booze."

"Booze?"

"Are you deaf or something?" She was starting to shout, "You know, booze, your favourite thing, stuff that makes you talk rubbish then throw up." She lowered her voice a fraction, "I presume it was, you know, smuggled," she saw my face again, "like that tobacco you buy down the pub."

"Don't bring me down to your level!" At last I was just angry, "How did you get involved with this? Don't you ever stop to think how stupid you're being. . ."

"Shut up!" She hit the cistern, "It was just some friends in London put me on to it, it's not a big deal. And anyway, that's irrelevant, the problem is that this time I didn't get paid."

It took a few seconds for it to sink in. "This time?" I whispered, "You mean you've done this before?" My lovely anger was fading, to be replaced by the nightmare certainty that this woman was a complete stranger to me.

"Yeah, a couple of times," her tone was suddenly defiant, "the money was good and. . ."

"When?" I could scarcely hear myself.

"What? Oh, when you played in Manchester that time, and when you were in Yorkshire."

Hell, I was crying after all.

"Kate," she faltered, "for heaven's sake, don't cry. I didn't want to worry you, and I knew you wouldn't approve. . . Kate. . ."

"Ooooow," I turned my head in misery to the wall, "can't you see how. . .how stupid you make me feel?" I was howling like a six-year old, "You let me go off thinking you're hanging out here, and all the time you're off making a fool of me with your. . .bootlegging." I tried to wipe my eyes.

"Oh Kate," she repeated a lot more softly, "it wasn't like that. Please, babe, don't cry, I didn't think you'd get so upset. All the same," she picked up steam again when I turned back sniffing to look at her, "I do get a bit bored sometimes when you go away. . ."

"Don't blame me!" Thank goodness, I was able to shout again, "You knew what my life was like when you moved up here."

Our argument was rapidly reaching its usual conclusion.

"No, I didn't! If I'd known what it would be like, I'd never have moved to this backward hole!"

"So fucking well move back south again," I shrieked and hurled a water-laden sponge at her.

She ducked neatly, and equally neatly caught the mirror it dislodged from the wall at the end of its messy flight.

"Good thing my reflexes are in working order," she remarked in her normal voice, putting the mirror tidily on the floor, "we could have had seven years of bad luck if it had broken."

"I think I'm already having it." I lay back in the bubbles and bobbed up almost immediately, "What d'you think you're doing?"

"What does it look like?" Her sliding grin emerged from her sweater as she pulled it off, "I'm coming in there with you."

"Oh no you're not," I crossed my arms over my chest, "I'm still really upset, I'm not in the mood. . ."

"Hm?" She stepped out of her jeans.

Dammit, I was lying.

"Ah darling," she displaced half the water in the tub, "I am sorry, truly, I never mean to upset you. . .I do miss you. . ."

Oh lord, she felt good.

"See," her voice was honey between her exquisite kisses, "you are in the mood after all."

"I've got a cunning plan," she said, scooping up a string of melted cheese, and licking her finger thoughtfully.

"Oh God." We were sitting up in bed, eating a delivered pizza, and I was having a little worry about whether the water on the bathroom floor would seep through and bring the kitchen ceiling down, and if it did, was it our responsiblity or our landlady's, a friend of Toni's who was in Australia. Another part of my mind was wondering how many times I could cope with going through the emotional mangle. Life was so unfair. Why did the most perfect lover in the world for me have to be such a monumental pain?

"Hang on," I thought I would jump in first, before she contributed further to my untimely demise from heart failure, "just tell me how you got mixed up in this. Who put you on to it?"

"Um. . ." She gave me her shifty look, "Actually it was a mate of Sylv's." She noticed that my jaws had ceased chomping. "Now don't go apeshit, I haven't spoken to Sylv for ages," her leg rubbed mine, "you know I'm not interested in her any more." Liz and Sylv went way back, and I trusted that cow about as far as I could spit. "And don't get all neurotic on me, jealousy's just a sign of your deep-seated insecurity, it's nothing to do with you and me and our relationship. Close your mouth, sweetheart, or you'll lose that prawn."

Just in time, before I battered her with the nearest blunt instrument, I realised she was laughing.

"You're horrible." I also knew that I lacked the energy for another fight, "Get on with it."

"OK," she munched a bit, "this guy, Baz, rang up and asked if I was interested, and when I said yes, he said this other guy, Jock, would ring me with the details, and he did."

"Jock?"

"Yeah, well, he was Scottish, but I'm making the massive assumption that it's not his real name. So he rang," she picked up a nice piece of squid lying on a slice I'd earmarked for myself and shoved it in her mouth, "and he told me where to go to pick up the van, where to go in Birmingham and boring things like that. Then he was the one who paid me when I got back to Scotland the first two times. Only this time, he just wasn't there, and eventually, I got pissed off with waiting and came home."

"Ah." I had the unmistakeable feeling that she was being less than frank, but I ignored it for the time being, "So why can't you ring Jock and ask him where he was?"

"Because he never gave me his number. And Baz doesn't have it either. Jock gets in touch with you, not the other way round. So I told Baz to ask Jock what he's playing at when he phones again, but so far, Baz hasn't heard a thing from him."

"Why can't you just let it go? And why do you always fall for these dodgy schemes?"

She looked shocked, "He owes me money! And," her expression changed to one of incredibly irritating complacency, "you know me, I like a bit of wheeling and dealing, it keeps me on my toes."

For an interval, I was at a loss for words. "So, what's your plan?" I looked round our familiar bedroom, and had a split second fantasy that I'd fallen out of the life intended for me into a parallel universe.

"Aha," she achieved the feat of looking more complacent, "it's a good one." She licked her fingers again, "Obviously, I wasn't the only person they used for driving the van on this run, and," she gave a self-satisfied sigh, "I think they always do the run on a Friday night. They must want the booze for a club or a party or something on Saturday nights. So I think we should pop up there this Friday night, or early Saturday morning, I suppose, and catch Jock when he turns up to pay this week's driver. I got there at about five in the morning yesterday, and you're only playing in Preston on Friday night this week, so that's plenty of time for you to come home, have a couple of hours kip, and then we can set off at about three. . .darling, careful, shall I hit your back?"

I had swallowed a lump of crust without chewing it. "Get your hands off me, you madwoman," I spluttered out between coughs, "I've never heard anything so. . .so insane in all my life."

"Glass of water?" She was unperturbed, "Of course, you know I'll go anyway whether you come or not."

I pulled at my hair. I was sure that there was less of it than a year ago. "But you can't go on your own, you might get hurt." Visions of her being cruelly assaulted, tied up and left in a lonely borders' barn afflicted me.

"So you'll come with me? But I haven't told you the best bit," she picked up the last bit of pizza, "I'm going to take Oscar."

"Who's Oscar?" A nightclub bouncer? A kung fu expert?

"Big Bertha's dog. He's a german shepherd cross, he's fucking enormous and he hates men."

That didn't surprise me, Big Bertha was about the most frightening woman I knew. "But you can't stand dogs. And how did you. . .?"

"NELS," she sucked some tomato contentedly through her teeth, "Big Bertha brought him along one week, we did some aversion therapy, and I'm fine with him now."

I digested this latest gem. I have never been remotely interested in involving myself in any kind of sporting activity, but I'd been aware of the existence of the somewhat grandly entitled North of England Ladies Softball club, well before I met Liz, and hadn't been too flabbergasted when she started going along to their winter training sessions. As far as I could tell, these mainly involved swapping filthy stories in a gym changing room, and I suspected that Liz was mostly looking forward to cutting a dash when they resumed playing in the spring. Of course, she would look beautifully slim and athletic compared with Big Bertha and Mighty Martha and the rest of the stalwarts. . .

"Well, are you coming with me or not?" In her underhand way, she had put one arm around me, and was giving my shoulder disturbing feathery caresses.

"I hate you."

"Good. It'll be fun." She smiled like a shark, and removed her arm to pick up a stray olive from the pizza box and press it gently into my mouth, "Chew it properly, my love." She skimmed the box on to the floor, "There's one little detail I haven't told you." She suddenly dived over the side of the bed, and started scrabbling at something underneath. There was a suspicious clinking. "Here," she emerged, slightly flushed, with two bottles of Belgian beer and a bottle opener, "since I didn't get my money, I did take a wee something for my trouble. A crate. Is your nose blocked or something? Your mouth's been open for ages."

I gave up. "My life was normal before I met you," I said weakly.

"Ah but babe," she fixed her naughty eyes on mine, "it was dead boring, wasn't it? Cheers."

"D'you think I'm a sex addict?" I asked Bill the next morning. We were in the recording studio again, this time for a singer neither of us rated. But we were getting paid, so we'd keep our mouths shut. He inhaled his vending machine coffee and snorted it out through his nostrils.

"Bloody hell, Kate," he said when we'd cleared up the mess with a handful of old tissues, "don't do that to me again. What makes you say that?"

"What d'you think? It's Liz, she can twist me round her

little finger."

"So that's what you girls do. . ."

I hit his knee.

"OK, ok, no, I don't think you are. I mean," he became a bit more serious, "it's like your drinking. You're not an alcoholic, believe me, I've worked with them. You don't drink every day, and I've never seen you play a gig drunk, but you do have a slight tendency to. . ."

"Binge?" I supplied helpfully.

"Something like that. So you're binging now, but you'll slow down after the first year."

"If we last that long." I was feeling pessimistic again.

He made another snorting noise, "Come on, it makes me nauseous to say it, but you're really well suited. Let's go, Golden Adenoids is here."

I followed him, a curious mixture of glowing happiness at his remark, apprehension that he was right, and terror that he was wrong warring within me.

The week was another relatively busy one for the band. We'd booked some studio space for ourselves to put together a new CD for the summer and had to spend time practising, to prevent the recording sessions degenerating into a series of missed cues and arguments over whose fault it was. I tried to concentrate, with the thought of Friday night lolling in the back of my head, while Liz, her good mood entirely restored, acted as if we were planning no more than a day trip to the beach.

"I suppose we should have an early night," she observed on Thursday evening, "but how about us nipping down to the Anglers for a quick one now? It's not raining or anything, and we haven't been out for a drink together for ages, what with the band and my classes and all."

"That's a nice idea," I said through a mouthful of chocolate cake, "it'll make a change from those stolen goods that're burning a hole in the bedroom carpet."

"Prude," the corners of her mouth twitched, "and don't eat all of that, I thought we could save some to maintain your blood sugar levels in the car."

"Am I getting fat?" This was another of my concerns since she'd installed herself in my kitchen.

"I like your curves," her smile expanded, "besides, it means I don't have to invest in an electric blanket."

Arms linked together, we walked companionably down the terraced streets, making rude comments about the decor of those unwise enough to leave their curtains open. See, I told myself, we can behave like a normal couple, maybe this'll be the last awful thing she does, Jock won't appear tomorrow night, nothing'll happen, she'll let it go and we'll settle down.

"No more than three drinks, now," she said bossily as we came through the doors into the warmth, "I'll get them in."

I didn't care. I sat near the fire with my back to the wall, smiling dippily at her rear view, and imagining myself to be the envy of every other woman in the place. Mine, all mine, heh heh, I cackled to myself.

"Kate! Didn't think we'd see you here, mind if we join you?"

It was Toni and, good heavens, she had Eleanor in tow.

"No, of course. . ." Liz, who hadn't met Eleanor so far, came back from the bar, and there were the usual introductions, "I've heard all about you" "It's all lies", offers of drinks and rearranging of chairs.

"Hey Toni," Liz, her hand resting on my thigh, turned to the expert, "what's the Socratic method of teaching then? I've been doing a bit of reading for my evening classes. . ." They settled down to some educational discussion, and, a bit taken aback by Liz's previously concealed academic leanings, I chatted with Eleanor.

"Haven't seen you for ages," she seemed a bit tired, and her voice was flat, "how's life?"

"Good, I think." I tried not to smirk too much, "You know, busy with the band and. . . things. How about you?"

"Yeah, really busy. I'm doing some work for the Bradley Action Group, it's getting quite interesting." She sipped at her apple juice.

She'd changed, she used to be a devil for the whisky.

"I've just signed their petition," I said proudly, glad to find some safe common ground.

"Good for you, the more local support and all that."

"Well, Ag made me," I confessed, and she smiled,

"I've a horrible feeling I'm going to be bailing some of her lot out of the nick, they're talking to all sorts of wild people on the internet."

She gave Liz a quick look and said more discreetly, "She's

31

nice. Any more of those where she came from?"

"God," I said, without pausing to connect my mouth with my brain, "I'm not a mail order bride service, Issy was asking the same thing the other day. . ." I stopped. "Hell, sorry, you and Amy aren't. . .?"

"Who knows," she slumped back, "probably just a bad patch, you know, we're both snowed under with work and . . ." she seemed to make up her mind about something, "don't seem to be on the same wavelength these days."

"It'll pass, I should think." I held back from observing that it sounded horribly like what had happened to Chloe and me. The confusing feeling that what was between us had been dislocated, the sensation of swimming through treacle, the inablility to express exactly what was wrong. . .

"After all," she was saying, "there's no rules about how your relationship should be. I mean, look at Toni and Lois."

"That's true." For years, Toni had been conducting this low key affair with a professor in London. She went down about one weekend a month, the two went on cultural holidays together, and they e-mailed each other every day, but Lois rarely made an appearance up here, and there had never been any hint that they wanted to live together, or see each other more often. "But I don't think that kind of relationship would suit me, though," I said, probably a bit more brutally than I should have done.

"You're just a romantic. So you've seen Issy recently. How is she?"

"Yeah, er, she seems to be getting on ok. I'm sorry, I didn't know if you two were communicating these days."

"Toni's always very tactful and doesn't talk about her, but I wouldn't mind seeing her. Looking back," her manner became more confidential, "I think I felt I had to stop being friends with her so I could stay with Amy but. . ." she stopped as Liz leaned our way to bellow romantically at me,

"Your round, podge, and don't get yourself a double while I'm not looking."

Still, when we got home after our regulation three drinks, I found myself coming over all soppy, and foolishly forgetting the torment behind and the probable terror ahead.

"It's nice being with you," I whispered as we tried to get our early night, "I suppose I'm quite glad I met you really."

32

4

Naturally, I'd changed my mind by one o'clock on Saturday morning when the band's van dropped me off at our door and I put my key in the lock. I was knackered and filled with nameless dread, and for more than a fleeting moment I wished I was tucked up in my old flat with a pot of tea, a good book and a hot water bottle. I turned the key, the window above me banged open, and Liz's yell rent the late night air,

"Kate! Stop! I have to. . ."

I had forgotten Oscar. A growling reminiscent of a jet engine limbering up came from behind the door, and I could almost feel hot breath and canine rage.

"Fuck." I leapt back, nearly losing my key down a drain in the process, and retreated to the other side of the street until Liz's head peered round the door.

"'S'ok. Come in and be introduced."

Muttering the worst words I knew, I recrossed the road and mounted our step. Practically the whole space between the front door and the stairs was taken up by a slavering mound of dog, restrained only by Liz's hand on a collar which would have served most normal sized men as a substantial belt.

"Oscar," Liz said in a weird sugary low voice, "this is Kate. She's a woman. Make friends now."

The dog mountain sank to its haunches and extended a bear like paw.

"Shake hands, Kate," Liz hissed a lot less sweetly to me, and, trying not to think of a promising career ended when those jaws met my wrist, I gave the heavy foot a brief clasp. He replied with what I assumed was a polite smile, and sank to the floor.

"Good dog," Liz patted his rough flank, "stay guard now." We squeezed past him into the sitting room.

"Isn't he something else?" She was happy as Larry, "Jock won't dare mess with us with him around."

"Will he fit in the car? He's like a three piece suite."

I put my instruments down and collapsed on to the settee.

Could I get away with not going, or would it be even more vile to stay here, not knowing what she was getting up to? "It was a cracking gig, thanks for asking."

"Sweetie, sweetie, cheer up," she knelt beside me and gave me a smoochy hug, "why don't you have a nice reviving bath, and I'll bring you up a cup of tea."

"How am I going to get up the stairs with that hellhound in the way?"

"He'll move for me." She ruffled my hair, "You can't fool me, I know you enjoy our little adventures really."

She ignored my frustrated remonstrances.

"One thing I can't decide," she said when she came into the bathroom with the promised tea, "is whether to give him his supper before we go or not."

"You mean you haven't fed him?" I sat upright, "Are you totally bonkers? He'll start on us, women or no women. Get my fiddle," I added, "and put it where he can't reach it. The attic or the roof, he might be attracted to the varnish."

"Well, I thought it might make him a bit meaner if he's peckish, though it does seem a bit unfair. I've got his supper, perhaps I'll just put it in the car, and we can feed him when we've sorted out our business."

"Your business." I drank some tea. "But will a whole calf fit in with him?"

"Oh Kate, it's only a tin and some biscuits." She was laughing all the same, "I think I'll make up a flask for us and get some blankets. We don't want to catch cold while we're waiting."

"Pneumonia would be a merciful release," I said, and handed her my mug, "get me another of these, would you, and Eleanor's number. I'm going to make a will. And don't even think of coming in here with me," I had seen the speculative look in her eyes, "I mean it, I need five minutes peace to contemplate the wreckage of my life."

"Five minutes, then," she swayed towards the door, "shall I make you a cheese and mustard sandwich as well?"

"Oooh yes." I forgot I was meant to be in despair, "But only if it's grainy. . ."

"You've got it." She left, and in spite of myself I grinned at her back.

In the end, I managed to doze for about half an hour before Liz's voice in my ear and her hand shaking my shoulder brought me out of a dream in which we were being threatened by kilted crowbar wielding Scotsmen.

"It's nearly three, babe, we'd better get going."

"I want my mum," I fell out of bed and began a search for my warmest clothes.

"You're right, you know," Liz observed once I'd put on woolly tights, a vast pair of cords, a thermal vest, two thick shirts and two jumpers, "you have put on a bit of weight."

"I think I'm just going to pretend I'm still asleep and this is a very vivid dream," I replied, "and I'll wake up on Saturday morning with some gorgeous young woman bringing me breakfast in bed."

"Quit moaning," she draped a scarf round my neck, "a change is as good as a rest."

Somehow we heaved and poured Oscar on to the back seat of the car, and set off through the silent streets. I made sure our bag of chocolate cake and other goodies was safely on my lap, way out of his slobbery reach.

"By the way," I asked as we left the city and joined the pitchy night motorway, "where exactly are we going?"

"You know Moffat?" Liz overtook a lorry with economical ease, the car, which never played up with her, an obedient extension of her long limbs.

"Yes."

"It's not really near there."

"Oh my." I had a little rustle in the bag to see what else she had put in, "If it's such a secret, why didn't you write the address down so I could memorise it and eat the paper?"

"That wouldn't do," she flicked her glance sideways at me, "if I told you, I'd have to cut your tongue out so you wouldn't betray me under pressure."

"You're so considerate."

"You're welcome."

I studied her firm profile and, driven by an impulse I didn't quite understand, leaned over and kissed her cheek. She put her left hand briefly on my leg, and I covered its smooth contours with my own.

"Why don't you have another sleep?" her voice was unusually kind, "I'll wake you up when we're nearly there."

I thought that overwhelming apprehension, the pungent

smell from the back seat and its accompanying whistling snores would make any sort of repose impossible, yet, still hugging our supplies, I must have sunk back into something resembling sleep, since the next thing I knew was Liz saying, "Nearly there."

I rubbed my eyes. I felt completely horrible. My mouth was dry, my head ached, my neck was stiff and my whole being revolted at the thought of what lay ahead.

'I think I want to die," I croaked, and wondered if a cigarette would improve matters or finish me off.

"Open up that flask, we'll have a swig of coffee." Her tone was detached, and I knew she had left me to concentrate on her self-imposed task. Swearing silently at her, I did what she said anyway, and, sensing the hot liquid inject a minute trickle of life into my system, I squinted out at the unfriendly night. Where the hell were we?

"It's just up here," Liz slowed down to swing up a narrow lane beyond an abandoned petrol station, and I sat getting sicker and sicker as we ground up a steep hill and then down the other side into what I presumed was a small valley. This was worse than the helpless terror I'd always suffered before violin exams, which had been about the biggest trauma of my childhood. I wished I was back in that hall, secure in the underlying knowledge that whatever happened, I would still be alive when it was over.

"That's the place." At the bottom of the hill, a concrete drive led from two gateposts, and we were going slowly enough for me to make out a sign fixed to one of them. "Kerrbank Mains", I read in the headlights.

"I'm going to go on up this lane a bit further. See if there's a good spot to park and look out for the van." Liz's voice was steady, and brooked no argument.

"What sort of place is Kerrbank Mains?" I ventured.

"Think it's an old farm, not worked any more. There's a yard and some converted barns used for a double glazing business and storage and stuff like that."

I shivered. This was no place to be in the small hours of a February night. We followed the lane as it rose again and bent to the right.

"Yeah, somewhere along here. We should just be above Kerrbank Mains. . .now." She pulled in at a gate set in a stone wall, "I looked at a map. This lane goes back to the main road a bit further on, which is handy." She turned off the engine and lights, "We'll wait here."

I couldn't think of anything to say. We sat in silence, and I stuffed my hands into my coat pockets while the temperature in the car dropped. Oscar panted and groaned, and Liz reached behind to give him a pat,

"Good boy. We'll have a walk in a bit."

An urge to weep came over me, and I set my jaw. I should have stayed at home, and left her to sort this out herself.

"Oh Kate," she was staring out of her window down into the inky valley, "don't worry. You know I'd never let anyone hurt you. If I really thought it was dangerous, I wouldn't have come, and I certainly wouldn't have brought you."

"Shit, you swine," I sniffled, "I don't know why I put up with you."

"Yes you do." She turned and I saw her quick grin, "Come on, let's have some more coffee and a nibble of cake."

Marginally restored, I didn't protest when, about ten minutes later, she pulled on her gloves, zipped up her leather jacket and opened her door,

"It's well after five now. Let's take a stroll down that field and get a bit closer to the yard. Move, Oscar, start earning your keep." She tugged at him until he flopped out on to the verge.

Cursing inwardly every inch of the way, I pulled an unattractive hat down around my ears, rearranged my scarf, got out of the car and lumbered towards the gate.

"How are we going to get that yeti over this? It's all chained up," I whined.

"We'll have to sort of lift him over the wall where it's a bit lower. That should warm us up." She looked along the wall, "There. It's not too brambly."

Working up a sweat, we pushed and shoved the recalcitrant monster over the wall without demolishing it entirely, and he stood on the other side, looking confused. It struck me that he wasn't the brightest of creatures.

"Stay," Liz commanded, and ran to the gate, then vaulted neatly over.

"Show off," I muttered, the odour of dog clinging to my gloves, and climbed over rather less sportily, hampered by

37

reluctance and the weight of my clothes.

"Buggerbuggerbugger," I chanted under my breath, stumbling after their indistinct figures until I joined them at a windbreak of ragged pine trees. Even in the dark, I could make out the low mass of buildings below.

"D'you think Jock is there already?" I asked. I couldn't see any lights on.

"Don't know. He might be waiting in a car somewhere. Stay Oscar." She took a firmer grip of his collar. He could obviously smell rabbit, and was doing his best to dislocate her shoulder.

"I wish you hadn't pinched that beer," I moaned, "I bet they noticed."

"All property is theft, as Marx said," she murmured absently.

"Proudhon," I corrected her.

"What?"

"It wasn't Marx, it was Proudhon. It's a common error, like people thinking Canute was trying to hold back the tide, when he was really trying to demonstrate that he couldn't, even though he was king. . ." I think it was the cold which was making me pedantic.

"What the fuck are you on about?" She must have been chilly as well, "Everyone knows it was Marx."

"Proudhon."

"Marx."

"Proudhon."

"Marx!"

"What do you think, Oscar?" I enquired. He was looking as if he had just realised that he hadn't had his supper and he wasn't at home with Big Bertha, dreaming of gnawing at male femurs and winning the favours of a pedigree red setter.

Liz closed her mouth like a ventriloquist. "Marx," she said in a growling bark, and started giggling.

A pair of headlights coming over the hill from the direction of the main road halted our juvenile chuckles. Nausea descended on me once more, and I let my teeth chatter while the lights descended, slowed and turned off down the drive, coming close enough for us to see that they belonged to a large transit.

"Right," Liz was tense again, "let's go for it. . ."

All hell broke loose. I nearly wet myself as a wail of sirens assaulted my ears, the yard came alive with flashing blue lights, and a voice, amplified by a loudspeaker, boomed into the air.

"Heuch ay polis nay bother ay customs and excise oot the van heuch ay surrounded," I made out.

"Fuck me, it's a bust," I'd never seen Liz so taken aback, "back to the car."

It was too late. Shielded by the windbreak, we were probably invisible to the forces of law and order below, but we couldn't miss the two police cars screeching triumphantly along the lane above us, no doubt anxious to join in the fun at Kerrbank Mains. Our prayers that they would overlook our innocent vehicle were in vain. One car came to an abrupt halt, lights revolving, behind the wall where we had left it.

"Fuck," Liz whispered again, her face drawn. Her life of minor transgression and this latest illegality had left her with a pathological distrust of the police, "I can't deal with this."

From nowhere, a wave of insane bravado came over me. "OK," I said in astonishingly commanding tones, "I'll sort them out. You and Oscar see if you can get back to that old petrol station on the main road without being seen. I'll pick you up when I can. But if I get arrested, I'll have to tell them about you. You can't just be left here."

She hesitated for a brief second, then shoved the car keys at me and was off, "I'll go through the fields," she said, and the night swallowed them.

Trying not to throw up, I struggled up the field, making a bargain with God that I would strive for a life of nun-like perfection if we got out of this hole. "Send me inspiration," I pleaded, and hauled myself over the gate to land at the feet of a policeman hewn from granite.

"Good morning, madam," he said, playing a torch over me.

"Good morning, officer," I replied politely, "whatever's going on down there?"

He ignored me, "Is this your car?"

I thanked the deity that I had won that particular fight with Liz, and it was my name on the precious ownership document, "Yes. Yes, it is."

"Can you tell me your name and address?"

I thought the better of lying, and stuttered it out, then watched him relay the information into his radio. I wished I'd had that SAS training which steels you to endure interrogation.

"Have you got your drivers' license, the vehicle documents and any other identification with you?"

I thought wildly. My license and everything else was in the chaos of my personal filing system back at the house. "No, sorry, no. . ." I felt in my pockets, "Hang on, all the car stuff is at home, what's this. . .?" I extracted a bent pass from some long ago festival, "I've got this. It's got my picture on." I handed it over and took off the hat which was obscuring most of my head. He examined it minutely in the strong beam of his torch.

"Very nice." He didn't give it back, "So, you're a musician. You're a long way from home. Could you tell me exactly what you think you're doing here?"

No! I almost shouted before launching into hysterical improvisation. "Well, um basically, I had a big. . .I had a huge row with my boyfriend tonight, so I. . .I just got in the car and started driving." I grasped at straws, "I used to come up to this area a lot when I was younger, and I thought. . .I thought it would make me calmer, and I've got friends in Edinburgh, so maybe I would have carried on. . ."

He appeared singularly unconvinced, and no wonder, "And could you tell me what you were doing down there?" He gestured towards Kerrbank Mains, from where bangs, shouts and grinding noises could be heard.

"I was just in the field. Er. . .call of nature, and then I started crying. . ." Perhaps my feminine vulnerability would soften his suspicious heart, "Then all that started, and I came back to the car."

"Oh aye." He took another look at my photo and then at me, "Just a minute, I know you, you play in that English band . . .Inertia Reel, don't you?"

Dumbstruck, I nodded. He spoke more quickly, "Hell, aye, I saw you in Peebles a couple of years back. You were supporting Fergus MacDonald." He named the greatest living fiddle player of our time. The gig had been the high spot of the band's career, and I suddenly forgot the trouble I was in, overtaken by a greater anxiety,

"Oh my, how were we? I was so nervous, playing on the same stage. I mean it was such an honour, with it being in Scotland, and us being English. . ."

"You were nay bad. But he's in another world, isn't he?"

"Oh yes." I remembered the ordinary looking man who had transported us to some rare place of communication with something greater, "It's like. . .it's like an angel takes over when he plays. . ." I stopped, before he thought of calling a police psychiatrist.

"Aye, he has the gift," his eyes were distant, "how do you think he rates compared with yon Irish lad. . .what's his name?"

"Mick Joyce?"

He nodded.

"Well, it's different styles, but if I had the choice, I'd listen to Fergus any day." This was the most bizarre conversation I'd ever had.

"So would I."

He brought himself back to the matter at hand, "It's cold out here. If I were you, I'd get in that car and go home to your man." He smiled, "Frostbite isn't going to improve your playing."

His radio crackled, and he recalled his duty, "It's not a good idea to go driving around willy nilly on a night like this. You get tired, and that's how accidents happen. You're lucky I'm not going to charge you with interfering with police business. We've enough trouble on without having to cope with upset lady motorists, nice fiddle players or no'"

"Thanks, officer," I quavered, thinking offers of free tickets to all our gigs for the next five years would be construed as bribery, and I fumbled my way into the driver's seat, stuffing the key into the ignition. "Start, you bastard lump of metal," I snarled. The engine hacked and whined, and I set smartly off, feeling the policeman's eyes boring into my back. He was going to change his mind, and decide I was the criminal mastermind behind the bootlegging, cunningly disguised as a bulky broken-hearted fiddle player. . .

Bowels aquiver, I reached the main road, and started panicking about Liz instead. She wouldn't have been able to slip past Kerrbank Mains without being spotted, the police would work out that she'd driven the van as well, Oscar

would go rabid and attack all and sundry, and my beloved
would be charged and sent to prison where big women with
tattoos would fight over her in the showers. I had just got on
to thinking that she would probably enjoy this part, when I
realised I was in danger of shooting past the petrol station.
I applied the brakes a bit too vigorously, and skidded across
the road on to the crumbling forecourt. Two shaking figures
emerged from behind the wrecked pumps. I opened my
door.

"Nice bit of driving," Liz commented, "good thing there are
no police within a hundred miles of here."

"What did the policeman say then?" she asked after we had
exhausted ourselves with siphoning Oscar into his place
behind us and she was pouring some coffee.

I set off at a more sedate pace, "He said I was right. It was
Proudhon, not Marx, so nah nah nah to you."

Her hands shook, the coffee went everywhere, and it was
a while before I had stopped laughing enough to drive at a
normal speed.

"Home, James," she said, wiping her eyes, "I've got
another little job lined up for this afternoon."

<u>5</u>

Fortunately, the little job was only taking pictures of a fence
which was starring in a neighbourly boundary dispute, and
I let myself believe that our alarms and excursions had come
to an end. Liz was suitably grateful for my part in saving her
from her just deserts, and I basked in her considerate
attention for all of forty eight hours. I slept for most of
Saturday, crawled out to a gig on Saturday night, and slept
again, so it wasn't until about one o'clock on Sunday
afternoon, when I was eating breakfast, that I was able to pin
her down to a serious talk.

"So what d'you think went down at Kerrbank Mains, then?" I asked.

"Have another piece of toast." She jumped up to the grill. I half expected her to start waving her arms around, saying things like, "Eat, eat, am I cooking my fingers to the bone for an anorexic or something," but she shrugged instead with the merest hint of her old indifference,

"I presume the customs and excise got on to Jock, and did a deal with the local fi. . .police."

Another worry had occurred to me, "But won't Jock, what is it you crims say, grass you up, if he's been arrested?"

"Why should he?" She dropped a golden brown doorstep on to my plate and sat down, "And even if he does, how interested are the police going to be if they've got him? I'm small fry." She stretched her arms luxuriously, then put her hand on the back of my chair, "Besides, driving a van in good faith isn't a crime."

"You're hopeless. I think you should carry Eleanor's number around with you all the time, for when you get to make that one call."

"Don't fret my little cabbage," Her hand moved, and her fingers reached the inside of my wrist, one of my many weak spots, "It's raining again. You can't possibly eat any more, why don't we go back upstairs?"

I pointed my buttery knife at her, "Only if you renounce your life of crime."

"For you, anything." I didn't believe her for a minute, but took advantage of her offer while the going was good.

The days grew imperceptively longer, and we slipped from dark winter to the beginnings of spring. No boys or women in blue appeared at our front door, and a fine Sunday afternoon in March saw us heading off to visit Issy.

"I have to go to a band thing in the evening, but the forecast's good, so why don't you bring Liz up for the afternoon, and we can have a little walk on the beach," she had offered on the phone the day before. I had been a bit wary of Liz's reaction to the promise of such innocuous and legal activity, yet she had agreed with something approaching enthusiasm,

"Sea air, just the thing, and I get to meet the famous Issy

at last, sure," she had said, running her motorbike chain through her hands, "you know, when I get this fixed, and the weather gets warmer, we can go off on the bike of a Sunday evening after the softball. Go to Devil's Bridge and hang out with the bikers, maybe even join a club. . ."

"Yes dear," I had replied, thinking she would be at least three relationships on by the time her poor bike was reassembled.

Issy lived in a little village outside Kirktown, and I gave Liz directions as we scooted along a road which skirted the bay, plunging through tangled woods and small fields arching down to the shore. Blackthorn blossom sprinkled the hedgerows, hawthorn buds were swelling, and celandines starred the verges. "Summer is icumen in," I warbled in my best soprano, "left here, no right. Right!"

"Women map readers," Liz swore and swerved up a minor road leading to the top of a sloping jumble of haphazard cottages and gardens.

"Oh wow," we said when we'd scrunched to a halt outside Issy's house and saw the view over the shining bay into Yorkshire, "wow," when we walked up her neat garden path bordered with crocuses and daffodils, "wow!", when we were ushered into her sitting room with its beams, plants and wood-burning stove. She had a dog as well, but this was an intelligent looking border collie, who surveyed us with bright eyes then waved his plumed tail.

"This is Tam," Issy said, "he doesn't bite."

"This is Liz," I replied, "she does."

"D'you want to swap?"

I liked seeing Issy smile like this, "No way." I had to be honest, "It suits me having someone around who can cook."

"Tam would bring you rabbits," she grinned, and Liz snorted,

"Before you finish bargaining, may I point out that I'm fully conversant with modern bathroom facilities, so you'd have to throw in the stove as well. I like your house, Issy."

"Thanks."

"You're a lot tidier than Kate, I must say. Maybe I'd consider a move."

I kicked her.

"Nice cup of tea?" Issy suggested, and I relaxed even more. It was all right for me to dislike Liz at times, but it would have been awful if none of my friends could stand her.

"Oooh, before I forget, Kate," Issy put her mug down a bit later on, "we've got some money through from Boltons, so I can pay you. Cash or cheque?"

"Cash," I said automatically, ignoring Liz's holier than thou expression.

"Tax dodger," she said anyway.

"It's white collar crime, it doesn't count."

"Why not?" I had actually succeeded in making her look startled.

"Because I'm highly unlikely to get caught." I took the notes from Issy and stuffed them in my pocket, "As long as I don't start driving around in a Porsche, I'm safe."

"You're out of control," Liz turned to Issy, "has she always been so dishonest?"

"I hate to disillusion you, but yes. I bet she's never told you about the time she. . ." she started on some ridiculous lie about my past. ". . .Mind you, she was very drunk at the time," she concluded, "don't be fooled by her air of girlish innocence."

Liz gave a dirty laugh, "I suppose the alarm bells should have sounded when she produced those handcuffs. . ."

"Shut up," I hit her with a cushion, "you promised not to tell anyone."

Liz subsided tittering, and Issy became more serious, "I'm glad you've got the money. There's a lot of weird rumours around town about Boltons. I know what they make is crap, but they keep most of the town in work. I've a horrible feeling Jeanie might be right, and they're going bust."

"Jeanie?" Liz who'd been fondling Tam's ears and gazing, dreamily for her, out of the window, came back to us, "Nice looking girlie with short fair hair?"

"Yerss. D'you know her?" There was a note of concern in Issy's question, as if Liz was going to tell her she'd seen her surrogate daughter in an S & M club, not that I was aware one existed in the city.

"Yeah, she's started coming to NELS, you know, the softball."

Issy looked relieved, "She's come over all environmental as well. She's really into this Bradley Action Group thing. Personally, I think she's chasing after some poor student who's in the group. She's my tenant," she added, for Liz's benefit.

"And a motorbike mechanic," I butted in.

Liz's eyes lit up, "I'll have to cultivate her." She gave me a glinting look.

"Cultivate away," I poked her with my toe, "you're far too long in the tooth for her."

"Right," Issy began clearing away the tea things, "I think you two need some fresh air before you get fractious."

We were halfway out of the front door, with Tam prancing ecstatically round our ankles, when we espied a short figure approaching the gate. Issy looked a bit embarrassed. "It's my neighbour, Jack," she whispered. "He looks after Tam in the day. I'll have to ask him to join us. D'you mind? Sorry."

"No problem," we made polite noises. "And we won't mention the handcuffs," Liz shouted.

"Afternoon, ladies," the old man lifted his flat cap, "off for a walk then? Nice day. Just passing."

"Come with us," Issy's voice was warm, "we're only going to the beach."

"Think my legs aren't up to a decent hike? You've never seen me and Tam run up Black Fell while you're dozing in your shop."

"Nuts. You just sit counting your money all day long and plotting how to get in with that Mrs Cowperthwaite down the village. No wonder Tam's getting fat."

"If you married me, like I keep asking, you'd soon get me fortune. I'd have a heart attack in a week."

"Keep asking. I've always wanted to be a rich man's plaything." They both cackled, and I realised that they had this conversation, or one like it, nearly every day.

We meandered back down towards the coast road, Jack entertaining us with a sociological run down of the inhabitants of the houses on the way,

"Mrs Butler, queer as Dick's hatband. . .He's away on the rigs, got another woman tucked up in Aberdeen, I reckon. . . Her daughter's expecting again, not the same father as the other three, of course. . .He's a crook. . ."

I stopped at a pair of gateposts topped by gilded carved lions. A drive led through manicured lawns and mature trees to an elegant Georgian mansion cloaked with creeper, the brass on its freshly painted front door catching fire in the sunlight.

"That's posh. Who lives. . ."

Jack startled us by giving a horribly vigorous hawk then spitting at the wrought iron gates, "Bastards. . .excuse me, ladies."

"Bolton House," Issy's eyebrows quivered, "Boltons bought it a few years ago, and they use it for entertaining high up executives and giving those boring management training courses. . ."

"Bah," Jack was evidently getting on his high horse, "they couldn't manage a scout troop. My pal," he fixed us with a beady look, "my pal, Mabel, she was a cleaner at Bolton's for years. Grand little worker, never missed a day, came and went like clockwork, and what did those bloody new managers do?" We shook our heads in ignorance. "Sacked her, that's what. Said she was too old and should, what did that letter say, 'Enjoy the fruits of her labours by taking advantage of their generous pension scheme'." He nearly spat again, "Broke her heart it did, she was dead in six months. Should have shoved their pension up their arses, beg pardon."

We were lost for words.

"Tainted money," Liz murmured behind my back, "you're dodging taxes on tainted money, you immoral thing."

"Tell you something, Jack," Issy took his arm, "I couldn't sleep the other night, and Tam and I were having a little wander around. . ." This didn't surprise me. Issy was a famous insomniac, who'd been known to ring people at three in the morning to ask for salad dressing recipes, ". . . Must have been about two o'clock, there were lights blazing, cars coming and going, I couldn't nip through the grounds like I usually do. What d'you think all that was about?"

He looked happier, "Top level crisis. Those greedy buggers should never have sold out to the Yanks. Global capitalism," he wagged his finger at us, "be the ruin of us all. I tell you," he smiled, "if I was younger, I'd be one of those, what d'you call them, New Age travellers. Yes, I'd sit around all day smoking cannibals raisins and playing a little whistle."

"You'd look nice with dreadlocks," Liz volunteered, "but you'd have to lose that cap."

"Hee hee. Maybe I'll just stick to training Tam to do his business on their lawn."

"Jack, you don't." Issy put her hand to her mouth.

"Just pulling your leg. Well, are we going to the beach or not? Always dawdling, you youngsters."

We crossed the coast road and followed another lane down to the shore. At the bottom, wedged between a low sea wall and a belt of rooky trees, was a small church, the angles of its thick stone walls and narrow embrasures softened by centuries of scouring winds.

"There was a village here once," Issy was giving us her local history lecture, "but there's some debate over whether it fell into the sea, or whether it was so badly hit in the Great Raid that they never rebuilt it."

"What's the Great Raid?" I asked, thinking it was an intelligent question.

Jack and Issy stared at me as if I'd asked who the prime minister was.

"You don't know?" Issy was as alive as I'd seen her for years, "When Robert the Bruce came down in 1322 and trashed the peninsula? I thought you had a history degree."

"Not my period," I mumbled, "and anyway, that was many vodkas and tonic ago."

"Well, he did. It was terrible and traumatic and the whole area was devastated. Houses burned, livestock stolen, crops ruined, masses of iron taken off to Scotland. They reckon the local economy collapsed, and it took years and years to recover, if it ever did."

"Ee, we suffered," Jack interposed gloomily.

"And what I always wonder," Issy led us down a tiny path to the beach, "is where all the feudal landlords were. Sitting in some safe castles far away, instead of defending the peasants, that's what I reckon. Especially the fat abbot of the local abbey. He was giving Robert the Bruce his tea while the hairy Scots ran wild. What a disgrace." She looked quite disgusted.

Jack winked at Liz, "Bet you didn't know we were all communists here. Come on, Tam, let's see if you can catch a seagull today." He stomped off to the water's edge, Liz at his elbow.

The beach was really no more than a wide shelf of shingle, but the tide was in, and the water was blue and dancing in the spring light. Issy and I stood on the rattling stones, looking at the city, golden and glowing as a fairytale place of promise, with the moors rising peacefully behind.

"God," Issy's voice had changed, "if I had a pair of good binoculars, I could probably see Mill Street. . ." She gave me a quick glance and lowered her voice further, "Kate; can I ask. . . how long did it take for you to get over Chloe?"

"Oh lord," I kicked at the rounded pebbles, "forever. Do you still. . .?"

"Well, I keep thinking I'm over Bel and everything, and then it all suddenly comes back and hits me, and I think I'm potty because it was all so long ago. And anyway," she looked embarrassed, "why did I find her sleeping with Amy such a big deal? Blimey, I've hopped into bed with women who had partners, and never thought twice of it. I'm mad, I'm sure."

"No." I touched her arm, "If you are, I was. I mean, even after I met Liz, I still felt something for Chloe." I sighed, "I think I really thought that we'd be together for ever, and it was such a shock to find out we wouldn't be. . .not that I'd want to be with her now, though. I don't know, it must be because we're middle-aged, but I'm beginning to think infidelity's a bigger deal than we make it out to be. . ." I let my eyes travel to Liz and Jack who were skimming stones across the wavelets, Tam skittering around them. They made an odd pair. Liz, tall in her black leather jacket and big boots, was bending her head to catch something that Jack said, and I saw her face crack into its lightening smile.

"Liz knew Bel," I said without pausing to consider where this might lead, "at college. They had a scene."

"Bloody hell," Issy almost choked, "talk about a small world."

"Mm." I felt my heart descend, "I think they're two of a kind really."

"What d'you mean? You don't think Liz'll do the same as Bel, do you?"

"Yeah," I knew this was the truth, "I think she will, sooner or later."

"Nah," Issy gave me a quick hug, "she loves you to bits, it's obvious."

"That's as maybe, but her track record's lamentable, and I'm always going away. . .your dog's having a swim." I was suddenly anxious to end the conversation.

49

"Bugger. He'll catch his death or get swept away by the tide. Don't encourage him, you little tinkers," she yelled at Liz and Jack, who were chucking lumps of driftwood into the cold briny for the dog to fetch, and we slid down to join them.

"I wouldn't come on to Jeanie, you know," Liz said out of the blue. The sun had set, and she was driving us home, her face unreadable in the gloom.

"Oh." I tried to suppress my delight.

"No, she's not my type," she said thoughtfully.

"Oh." I was deflated.

"No," her tone was ruminative, "I seem to be going more for the pathologically jealous musician type these days. . . Let's go cross country!" Without warning, she yanked at the steering wheel and spun us down a grass covered track.

"Jesus! What are you doing?" I rubbed my shoulder where the seatbelt had dug into me.

"I noticed this on the way here." She slammed on the brakes at the edge of a little copse, "Well?" I saw she was laughing, "I'm not too long in the tooth to get enterprising on the back seat. What about you, Curly?"

How could I have refused such a romantic gesture?

Neither of us heard the phone when it rang later that night. This was because we were having a heated debate about song lyrics in the bath. It had started harmlessly, with Liz crooning agreeably to me while we soaked away the strains and odd bruises brought on by our attempt to rediscover our misspent youth, but spiralled downhill once she had launched on her rendition of "Will you still love me tomorrow?".

"You always do that," I nitpicked when she had paused to draw breath, "you muddle up the words, and sing the last two lines of the second verse in the first verse, and the last two lines of the first in the second."

"I don't!" she splashed me.

"You do," I splashed her back.

"I do not! I know this song backwards."

"Yeah, and that's the way you sing it. . .not the showerhead! Think of our water bills!"

After midnight, I was nearly asleep when she started up again.

"Tonight you're mine completely," her low voice insinuated across the pillow into my ear.

"Right!" I shot bolt upright, "I've got that tape downstairs somewhere." I put on the light, "I'm going to find it right now and bring it up here and play it to you, so you learn the error of your ways." I stuck my arms into a bathrobe and flounced out of the room, seeing out of the corner of my eye that the quilt was heaving over her shoulders. Downstairs, I surveyed the heaped sitting room and pondered. Where were my old tapes? I absentmindedly lifted a sheet of music from the answerphone and saw the winking light which hadn't been there when we went upstairs. My insides lurched. At this time of night, it had to be bad news. My nieces, Liz's mum. . . I pressed the button and heard Ag's voice, young and scared under its customary aggrieved brusqueness,

"Liz, Kate, be in please. I'm in the phonebox at Upper Barton. Come and get me, I'm dying out here. . ."

6

At my screech, Liz came flying downstairs, baseball bat in hand.

"What? What?" She looked around wildly for someone to bash, "Is it a burglar?"

Even with no clothes on, she would have frightened most self-respecting intruders.

"It's Ag," I pointed at the answerphone, "she's in some sort of trouble. Listen."

She hefted the bat from hand to hand while I replayed the message, "I'll have to go and fetch her."

She dropped the bat on to the settee, "What time did she phone? Have you done 1471?"

I shook my head.

"I bet it's not that serious, she'll have got drunk and missed her lift or something. Don't look so scared." She leant over

51

and pressed the numbers, sloped to the kitchen to look at the wall clock and came back with the car keys, "About an hour ago. Suppose I'd better nip out and see if she's still there."

"I'm coming with you. Are you going like that?"

She rolled her eyes, "Of course, nude driving is my speciality. You don't have to come, get some rest." I was meant to be in the studio at some ungodly hour in the morning.

"I'm coming." I repeated, "Who knows what mischief you'll get up to without me."

"It's so nice to be trusted," she headed off up the stairs, and I followed in her wake, fighting an urge to bite her ankles until she admitted she was worried.

We dressed in silence, apart from the odd "That's my sweater," and "Pass those socks," and clomped out to the car.

"D'you know where Upper Barton is?" I asked as she ground out of the parking space, nearly taking the bumper of the car in front with us.

"Of course." She revved up and blasted us to the end of the street.

"Well, you're going the wrong way," I pointed out helpfully, once I saw we were heading in the opposite direction.

"This is a short cut," I made out between her clenched jaws.

"Yeah, to Manchester maybe," I persisted, "Upper Barton's to the north." And not a million miles from the Bradley development site, I realised belatedly.

She stamped on the brakes, "You drive then, know-all."

We swopped places, and I set off rather more sedately, thinking futilely that she could have thanked me for coming along and saving her from a night of driving round in circles. She kept her mouth clamped shut until I had turned off the main road and was threading through the winding lanes, and she saw the sign for Upper Barton in the hedgerow.

"OK, don't say anything," she muttered, "I was confusing it with Bridgetown." I was sure she'd made that up, I'd never heard of the place. "Where's the phonebox, then, clever clogs?"

"Near the church," I said smugly, slowing down to

negotiate the one main street of the village. I only knew this because about ten years ago I'd played for a barn dance in the village hall, then enjoyed a lock-in in the pub, and had a vague memory of Chloe and I snogging in the phonebox while we tried to ring for a taxi back to the city. I must have smiled at this happy thought, because she jabbed me with her elbow,

"What's so funny?"

"Nothing," I lied. "Look, there it is. . .damn, there's a van where I want to park. Hope it's not poachers. Can you see Ag anywhere?"

"It's dark, you ninny. Why don't you pull in on the verge here. . . yeah, and just demolish that historic lych gate while you're at it."

"Piss off." I parked close enough to the churchyard wall to make it impossible for her to get out of the passenger door, rolled a cigarette, stuck it in my mouth and lit it, then condescended to open my door and step out into the placid rural night.

"You'll kill us both with your driving," Liz said unkindly, easing herself over the handbrake and pulling herself out to stand beside me.

"Bollocks. I'm a much safer driver than you. I don't go half so fast." I started walking in the direction of the phonebox.

"You're not. You lack confidence, and that makes you dangerous."

"So, it's over confidence that causes accidents. All those boy racers think they're good drivers, and then they go and run over old ladies on zebra crossings." I sucked on my cigarette.

"I've never run over an old lady in my life," she drew level to me, "though I might make an exception in your case."

"I'll watch out for you when I'm off to the shops with my zimmer frame. . ." I could tell she was beginning to smile, and our pace slowed as she put an arm round my shoulder, then drew us to a halt.

"You're so annoying," she said softly, her fingers taking my cigarette and throwing it away. In spite of the cold, we kissed very slowly, the nape of her neck strong and vital under my hand.

"Give it a rest, you two," a familiar voice halted us in mid-flow, and we gaped at the two figures who had materialised from the van.

"Issy! What are you doing here? Hello, Tam," I bent to pat his bouncing back.

"I got a frantic call from Jeanie. It's taken me an hour to get here, I got lost." Issy's tone matched her worried frown.

"We got a call from Ag about the same time, but we missed it. . .," I saw the changed look on her face, "we were arguing, thanks very much."

"Where are they then?" Liz peered around, "Hiding in the graveyard so they can jump out and scare us? Or d'you think they've buggered off, the little toe rags, I'm missing my beauty sleep."

The three of us stood blankly, absorbing the fact that there was no discernible sign of life in the sleeping hamlet.

"Tam'll find them if they're here," Issy's confidence was heartening, "Tam," his ears pricked up like aerials, "go find Jeanie!" He pointed his nose as if he was auditioning for a remake of Lassie, gave a quivering yelp, danced around for a few seconds and plunged through a black hedge on the other side of the road.

"Shit." We stared at the thorny impenetrable barrier.

"Let's walk along a bit, see if there's a gap further on," Issy was being practical. "What can they be up to, at least Jeanie didn't take my van this time."

"Ag sounded a bit scared, which isn't like her," I said, shivering in the wind which had built up since this afternoon, "maybe it's something to do with this Bradley thing, it's not that far from here."

Our footsteps were loud, and a drop of rain hit my cheek. "Why do I always end up traipsing around in the middle of the night?" I grumbled to Liz, a bit more quietly, "this never happened before I met you."

"I told you not to come," she didn't sound too thrilled either, "but you never listen to me."

"That's because you're so full of it. . .Issy," I raised my voice, "what are the words to 'Will you still love me tomorrow'?"

"What?" She saw us scuffling, "I'm keeping out of this. How about here?"

We paused at a sort of gap, patched up with bits of wood

and chicken wire.

"Let's give it a whirl," Liz stopped pulling my hair, "I hope Tam hasn't got the wrong end of the stick and is off courting at some farm. I can't hear him."

"He's a silent and deadly tracker," Issy struggled through the hedge and we blundered after her, "some of the time, anyway. Mind that wire."

We emerged, with various ripping and cursing noises, into a field. Even in the cloudy night, it didn't take long for us to realise that the farmer had been muck spreading, probably that very day.

"Lovely," Liz looked down at her boots, "I just hope it's farmyard manure, and not from a septic tank." The rain got steadily more persistent.

"Should we shout?" I was sure I could see what looked horribly like shreds of loo paper on the ground.

Issy put her fingers to her mouth, "I'll give him a whistle. . ." At her words, barks and cries floated towards us from the far side of the meadow, and a couple of minutes later, a tall shape followed by two shorter ones, their arms around each other, loomed up in front of us.

"Ag?"

"Jeanie?"

"Where were you?" There was no mistaking Ag's dulcet tones, "I phoned bloody ages ago. . ."

"Hello, darlings," Jeanie's beaming face showed no sign that this was anything but a routine meeting, "hi, gorgeous," she winked at Liz.

We set about them like a bunch of angry parents.

"What were you thinking of, calling us up like this from the middle of nowhere. . ."

"You're the limit, you're not having the van again. . ."

"Do your mum and dad know about this? I've been worried sick. . ."

"Shut up!" Ag and Jeanie yelled simultaneously, "you're not my mum!"

The heavens opened.

"Shall we go back to the cars?" I suggested, "so we can discuss stopping your pocket money in the dry?"

"Please." Jeanie's companion, who had been silent so far, gave a desperate wail, and Jeanie hugged her closer.

"Don't give us a hard time," Jeanie suddenly looked furiously protective, "we've been doing our bit for the environment, and she's bloody freezing." She bent her head, "'S'ok, babe," she murmured in her loved one's ear.

Issy groaned, "Oh come on, you silly things, I've got some dry coats and coffee in the van, and I don't think Tam ate all the biscuits. . ." She guided them back towards the gap with Tam, his mission accomplished, trotting complacently at her heels.

"Who's she?" Liz asked Ag in a stage whisper.

"Her new girlfriend, Alison. I've had to listen to them canoodling for hours." She snagged herself on a jagged barb of wire, "God, could you find a harder way to come round to us? There's a gate opposite the churchyard."

"Do you want us to leave you here?" I'd never heard Liz speak to Ag quite so sharply, "And you'd better tell us what you've been up to."

"Sorry." This was about the first time I'd heard her apologise as well, "Can I tell you in the car, I'm a bit cold."

"Blimey, you're the end," Liz took her arm, and we squelched up the lane to the vehicles. Refusing Issy's offers of coffee and biscuits, we said some hasty goodbyes, and piled into the car.

"Here," Liz found a rug on the floor, "put this round you."

"Ta. . .wow, it's a bit smelly, have you had a dog in here?" She huddled up in it all the same, and I turned the unreliable heater on full.

"All right," she said, once we were heading safely back towards the city, "we were doing something for BAG."

"What, a midnight sponsored walk?" Liz was sceptical.

"Oh don't be like that," she blew on her hands, "we did some direct action."

I glanced at her through the rearview mirror, "You don't look like you've been tunnelling. Have you been building itsy bitsy tree houses?"

"I don't know why I didn't call mum and dad. You two are getting nearly as bad, just listen for a change." I wondered if I had been like this twenty years ago. She huffed and puffed a bit, "We got word, and I'm not telling you how, that Bradley's were starting work on the site this weekend. Surveyors and stuff. So we thought we'd nip along early this evening, and take a look, and then. . ." She sounded like she did when she was debating with herself whether to trust us with some nefarious secret, "We saw all their markers and things, and there didn't seem to be anyone about, so we decided to just. . .rearrange them a little."

"Ag, you vandal," Liz was delighted, "you'll be chaining yourself to a bulldozer next."

"Does Eleanor know about this?" I stayed in strict parent mode, "It'll make it hard for her if half of you are breaking the law all over the place. Did you think of that?"

"Don't be a wet blanket, Kate." Ag was recovering rapidly, "Anyway, that's not all, we were really getting into it, when all of a sudden," her voice got faster and more excited, "these redneck security men appeared from nowhere and charged into the field."

"Oh my God, Ag," I swerved a bit close to a wall, "you could have been hurt."

"Well, we ran," she was starting to giggle, "we ran for the woods, and me and Jeanie and Alison ended up together. We hid for ages in case the buggers were still around, and when we came out, we found all the others had gone, the rats, so that's when we went to the phonebox. We've been in some sort of shed, we nearly died of exposure."

"Would have served you right," I said severely, dropping to the speed limit at the city approaches, "shall we take you to your house, then?"

"Yeah, I can sneak in. I'm grateful really, you know, I've never been so cold."

"Have a nice hot mug of cocoa, and contemplate our self-sacrifice," I instructed slightly more sympathetically, "I suppose we couldn't have left you there, my conscience might have bothered me eventually."

"Aw come on, Kate," Liz poked my leg, "admit it, you were dead worried." She turned to the back, "She cares for you very deeply, she just doesn't want to say it."

"Get knotted, the both of you." I stopped outside the house in which, in retrospect, I'd spent some very calm years, "Let me know if that new tenant moves out, Ag, I might consider a move back."

"I believe you." Ag leaned forward, and I could see she was giving us one of her rare smiles, "Thanks, girls, I owe you one." She got out of the car, and we watched her creeping up to the door and, with the ease of practice, slipping noiselessly inside.

"Never a dull moment," Liz's twitching smile had reached her eyes, "let's go home, auntie."

I had a dark foreboding that this wasn't going to be the last we heard of the Bradley development, and that this wasn't going to be an isolated escapade. Why couldn't everyone stay at home around the piano and make their own entertainment these days?

Busy with the band for the next few weeks, however, I had another cloud on my horizon. This year we had planned a repeat version of a tour we'd done three years ago, and would be away from the beginning of August until the end of October, apart from our annual break of a week in September, wowing audiences from the north of Scotland to Germany. All through the winter, the tour had remained comfortably in the future, and Liz and I had never discussed it, yet now, with spring in the air, it was getting ominously close. I found myself dreading mentioning it. It was hard for me to imagine Liz knitting placidly and faithfully at home while I popped back for the odd night here and there. She wouldn't be able to afford to come away with us, even if she wanted to, and I was trying to stop thinking that it was in her mind that this would be a convenient point at which to pack her bags and leave. Not that she gave any hint that this was her intention as we carried on in our usual vein of fitting in our bickering, about nothing, and making up, around our separate working hours. She had got well in with a photographer who had more jobs on than he could handle, and even, to her shame, went off to photograph a couple of weddings.

"Was it lovely and romantic? Did you cry?" I asked one Saturday afternoon when she had come back from such an outing and was stretched out on the settee, her face broadcasting that she had reached the end of her admittedly limited tolerance and patience.

"Have we got any beer? That was a fucking nightmare."

"Good frocks?" I found a can I'd been hiding for myself behind the log basket, "Sorry it's not cold."

"It'll do." She popped the top and cursed again as the

lukewarm froth surged down her chin and on to her neat white shirt. She was wearing some smart black trousers as well, and I began to regret that I was meant to meet up with the band in approximately ninety minutes, and that she was not in the best of moods.

"Great frilly lacy things," she moaned, "with nasty bratty bridesmaids, and all the groom's lot were pissed. They'll be divorced in two years, what a waste of money and effort. Jesus." She drank some more, "Off to Carlisle then?"

"Yep." I squinted down a whistle to check it wasn't full of fluff."

"Coming back tonight?" Was this an innocuous enquiry? Why was I so suspicious all of a sudden?

"Hope so. It'll be late though." Dammit, I wished we were playing in town.

"I won't wait up." She sighed, "What you doing tomorrow afternoon?"

"Nothing definite. Why?"

She kicked her legs, "First game of the season for NELS. Big grudge match against a bunch of women from Leeds." She sighed again, and said in a voice that I realised wasn't as casual as she would have liked, "Come and watch?"

"D'you want me to?" I pinged my violin strings, checked I had some spares, and put the case near the door.

"Wouldn't ask if I didn't." She scrunched up the can and tossed it with laid back accuracy into the bin, then leant her head back and shut her eyes.

You're horrible, I thought, you could be more pleasant sometimes. I brushed past her to get at my boots which had somehow made their way into the corner, and tried not to notice how desirable she was. Then I gave up. Some things were more important than obsessive time-keeping, and, as I told her when she'd stopped struggling, it was her fault for dressing so provocatively.

I was only five minutes late for the van, and the next afternoon saw me sitting loyally in the park waiting for the action to begin. I hadn't expected such a social gathering. It wasn't particularly sunny, but it was mild for April, the park cafe was open, and groups of women sat around the outside tables or on the grass, eyeing up any new talent among the visitors from across the Pennines. I had left Liz to her pre-match team bonding which, from the ululations and blood-curdling yells coming from behind the cafe, was not for the faint-hearted, and was carrying a mug of tea out from the cafe counter when I saw Toni and Eleanor laughing over something at one of the tables. There was no sign of Amy.

"Kate!" Eleanor had seen me, "Come and sit down. I was just telling Toni about your mercy dash to retrieve Ag last month."

"So she told you then." I scraped an iron chair closer to the table, "Isn't it a bit of a problem for you, being BAG's legal eagle and everything?"

"Officially, of course, I know nothing about it, and would never support such impetuous and illegal activity," she sounded perfectly relaxed, "but as an individual, I can only applaud their principled stand against the rampant forces of unbridled commercialism. . ."

"She's rehearsing posh sentences for when she's on the evening news," Toni interrupted, "I'm lending her my dictionaries."

"You never know," Eleanor looked like a cat which has discovered a side of salmon in an unguarded pantry, "I've found out something really interesting about the land right next to the Bradley site. . ." her voice faded, and her face gradually stiffened. Intrigued, I followed her eyes to see Issy, Tam by her side, walking hesitantly towards us.

<u>7</u>

Both Toni and I shrank back in our chairs, nervous leers plastered on our faces. I recalled that, in her worst state, Issy hadn't held back from blaming Eleanor for not keeping Amy under control, and I had a feeling that Eleanor had thought, however unfeasible it might seem, that Issy should have done the same with Bel. Was this going to be a long-delayed showdown, with shouts and screams and flying crockery?

Then Eleanor gave an odd muffled groan, rose to her feet and ran towards Issy, enfolding her in a huge embrace. I caught the look of delighted surprise on Issy's face, before Toni and I turned politely to each other, leaving the two to huddle together in relative privacy.

"Nice and warm for the time of year," I blurted.

Toni's grin was relieved, "Thank God," she fanned herself with a napkin, "four years I've had to try and keep them apart, and now I can stop. Maybe even Issy and Amy will kiss and make up."

I bent closer to her, "So where is Amy? What's going on with her and Eleanor?"

"El said that she was working today," Toni became reflective, "I don't know, I can't imagine them not being together, it would be such a shame if they can't work it out. . ." She stopped as Issy and Eleanor, wreathed in smiles, sat down at the table.

"Jeanie dragged me here," Issy explained, "her beloved is writing an essay." She patted my shoulder, "Come to watch your sexy squeeze then? Stopped smooching long enough to hold her half-time orange?"

"Is it true they're not allowed to do it the night before a match?" Eleanor asked.

"Of course not," I said without stopping to think, and then blushed horribly as a mental flashback to the pleasant morning Liz and I had spent together collided with the view of three sniggering faces. "You're all so vulgar," I pouted, "I'm going to concentrate on higher things. More tea, anyone?"

We settled amicably down to watch the match, with Eleanor and Issy's murmuring efforts to bring each other up to date after four years' separation burbling along in the background. I had to admit that I didn't have much of a clue as to the rules of the game, although I worked out that the visitors were batting first. From where I sat, it looked like an infinitely more aggressive version of the rounders games we used to play at primary school, with a lot of shouting at the unfortunate referee, ill-tempered jostling on the bases and snidey titters from the Leeds team crouched together on the grass, mainly directed at Big Bertha and Mighty Martha who were positioned like geological formations on two of the bases. Jeanie, her features set in an expression of unlikely and fierce seriousness, was doing most of the bowling, which seemed to involve an endless variety of hand signals and winks, and, after a while, I gave up trying to work out if we were doing well, and concentrated on watching Liz slinking around the outfield in a natty dark tracksuit. Her moment of glory came when, after a hefty Leeds lass had given the ball a mighty crack, she ran fluidly sideways and leapt into the air like Superwoman to catch the ball as effortlessly as if it had been travelling in slow motion. Almost in the same movement, she sent the ball in a swinging arc back to Jeanie, before swaying round so she could see me. The look of undiluted pleasure on her face made me catch my breath, and I had to stop myself from tearing over and flying into her arms. But soon after, it must have been half-time, she was loping towards us, her hair ruffled and her cheeks flushed.

"Hi ladies, hello sweets," she sat on my lap without preamble, burying one hand in the curls at the back of my head. "Did you see me?" she asked quietly, her eyes fixed on mine, her lips parted in a half-proud, half self-mocking grimace.

I forgot about the others. "You're beautiful," I whispered, and pulled her closer, inhaling her familiar scent of soap and warm body.

"Oh God," she broke away eventually, "we'll frighten the horses. I don't think this is part of the half-time pep talk." She looked around, "And here comes our little star, lowering the average age of the team to below forty."

Jeanie was trotting in our direction, a ten pound note clutched in her hand.

"You're too old for that sort of thing," she shouted, "want anything from the caff?"

"Coke and a mars bar?" Liz shouted back, and then shifted on my lap, putting her mouth to my ear, "I'd better give her a hand. I love you. See you after a bit."

"Good luck." Something odd had happened to my voice, and my view of her jumping up the step into the cafe was blurred. Outside the heat of passion, we hadn't said this to each other very often. I blew my nose, and attempted to bring myself back to earth.

". . . I'll have to check on this," Eleanor was saying, "but it looks like there might be a loophole in the land deal Bradley's did."

Jeanie's head popped out of the cafe door, "They're all owned by the same group, you know, from America."

"What?" Issy and Eleanor started at her apparent non-sequitur.

"Just a mo'," her head disappeared and then she and Liz came out bearing laden trays. "Boltons in Kirktown who make margarine and Bradleys," Jeanie continued as if it was patently obvious, "they're all part of the same business." She set off back towards the softball team, frowning at her wobbly burden, with Liz in her wake.

"Hang on," Eleanor yelled after her, "how d'you know that? Stop, speak to me. . ."

"Everyone knows," she risked a look back over her shoulder, "catch you later if you want to chat."

"Could she be wrong?" Eleanor turned to Issy, "How would she know a thing like that? I thought the Bradley people were based in Manchester, from the research I've managed to do."

Issy shrugged, "Practically all her relatives either work for Boltons or have done, she always seems to know the gossip. Is it important?"

"I'm not sure," Eleanor was thoughtful, "it might be." She looked at me, "Nice to see a couple so in love and so restrained in public as well."

"Sarky." I had reverted to believing my life was perfect, "What's this about a loophole?"

"Oh ho ho," Eleanor grinned remarkably evilly for a respectable solicitor, "this could be good fun." She launched into exposition. "Bradleys bought the site, which was just pasture mainly, from one of those companies which owns lots of farms. But the neighbouring farm is a family run affair, and the farmer's a good egg, very right on and thinking of going organic and stuff. So he's not too keen on the development, and got in touch with me when Bradleys asked him if they could lease a strip of his land next to their site for access and things like that. It's got another gate on to the road, and it'll make it easier for them." She leaned forward and stabbed the table, "The point is, he told me that

63

that bit of land technically isn't his at all. No indeed, it used to be common land, and his farm have rented it at a peppercorn rent from the local parish council for generations. So." For an instant, she looked as complacent as Liz in one of her smugger moments.

"So?" I was bewildered.

"Don't you see?" She waved her arms around, "It's common land, the parish council are opposed to the development, not, I may say, like the district council who have been in effect bribed with the promise of jobs and improved roads, and the farmer wouldn't get too aerated if a few environmentally conscious citizens decided to wander down and keep an eye on what the developers are doing, check they're not breaking their planning restrictions and squashing too many daisies or whatever."

"Ah," the cogs in my brain were finally beginning to move, "you mean if people went down there and perhaps missed the last bus home and had to stay overnight, and the farmer came to the conclusion that he couldn't possibly let heavy equipment on to that bit of land anyway. . ."

"Exactly." Eleanor's face was wolfish, "It probably won't stop the development in the long run, but it'll make it awkward for Bradleys, and perhaps make similar firms think twice, if they've got a nice big protest camp right in their faces."

"Good Lord," Issy's eyebrows shot upwards, "you mean we might have our very own Greenham Common?"

"Well, maybe," Eleanor smiled at her, "If anyone wants to take this up."

"Ag and her mates will love it," I claimed. "They can miss college and say it's all in a good cause. And you'll get all those odd bods who live in the woods, and all the old hippies, and anyone who turns up from outside."

"Won't the council just clear them all off?" Toni was being sensible.

"Eventually yes." Eleanor had obviously thought it all out, "But if the parish council and the farmer don't object to people being there, we could spin it out for ages. . .Jesus!" A ball clanged against the table, rattling our cups. The game had restarted, and that had been Mighty Martha's effort.

"Don't help them!" Issy put her hand on Eleanor's arm to

stop her retrieving the ball and tossing it back to the puffing Leeds fielder who was heading our way, and we sat like statues while the poor woman grovelled around our ankles, giving us filthy looks. It didn't do us much good, however. In the end, our home team managed to lose, due, I gathered, to a fatal combination of the larger women's less than agile running between bases, and injury to our key player, namely Liz.

"Look," she said to me, rolling up her trouser leg to reveal a livid raised bruise as we joined the dejected group and ignored the raucous celebrations behind us, "I think that foul woman has broken my shinbone."

"What happened?" I asked unwisely.

"Didn't you see it?" She snorted, "She tripped me up on purpose when I was running for second base. I thought you were meant to be watching, what kind of girlfriend are you?"

"A devoted one." I took her arm, "Come home and I'll kiss it better."

"Promise?" Her hand slipped into mine.

I made a snap decision that this softball idea was turning out to be an unlikely blessing, "I promise. And I'll make you a jelly for tea, to make up for it."

"OK," her laughter gurgled in her throat, "I'll hold you to that. Let's go soon. We were all going to go for a drink, but I don't think I can face a post mortem yet." She limped forward a step, "I'll just say goodbye to everyone and pick up my stuff. . ."

I stayed with Toni while the afternoon broke up, aware of Issy and Eleanor engaged in an intense conversation a few yards away.

"I wasn't sure at first," Toni said suddenly, "but I think you're on to a good thing there."

"Oh." I gave her a sidelong glance, "I just don't want to. . . you know. . . have too high expectations."

"You worry too much, you'll be fine. . ." she broke off as Jeanie bounced up to Issy, and Eleanor drifted back in our direction, "I'll have to have a proper supper party sometime, and we can all get together. I think I'm giving Eleanor a lift home, see you soon, lovey."

"See you. . ." I waited for Liz, then we walked peacefully home through the domesticated Sunday streets, with me chewing her ear about the likelihood of BAG's getting it together to set up a protest camp, and whether we would have to rescue Ag from a dawn raid by council bailiffs.

"You know why this house is always a mess of course," Liz said that night, propping herself up on one elbow to look down at me.

"Oh, why?" I stopped counting her ribs, and let my fingers rest in the entrancing hollow above her hips.

"It's because when we happen to be here together, we spend all the time doing this."

"Do you mind?" My hand tensed, and I could feel myself starting to frown.

"No," I was able to read only amusement in her expression, "You know it's my favourite hobby. But," she changed position to lie on her back staring at the ceiling, "it's nice having you around for things like this afternoon as well. I mean, I knew you'd be away a lot when I moved up here, but I suppose I didn't really think what it would actually be like."

Shit. I couldn't think of what to say, we rarely had deep and meaningful conversations. And I was going to Wales on Tuesday for nearly a week, and the tour wasn't about to go away...

"God, Liz," the words came out before I could stop them, "I'd leave the band and get a job, if that's what you wanted." Had I gone completely insane? That was the last thing I should do.

"You daft bag," she rolled over and hugged me, "you couldn't do that, you're unemployable. Don't mind me, I'm just having a touch of Sunday night blues." Her legs enfolded mine, "And stop agitating about that bloody tour as well, we'll work something out." She could read my mind, too.

"But Liz," for some reason I couldn't let it go, and succumb to our usual method of solving problems, "I don't want you to be unhappy here. I love you." There, I had said it.

"And I love you. I'm not unhappy. What's the problem?"

The problem was that I had gone stiff as a board, and had the unnerving sensation that an unsounded abyss was opening up under our feet.

"I... I just don't want..." I started stuttering. My

customary response to her advances was completely absent.

She withdrew from me and sat up, her shoulders hunched. "I know what this is about," her voice was detached, "you think I'm going to start sleeping with other women when you're away, don't you?"

I thought about lying, but knew I couldn't, and she recognised my agonised "Mm" as assent. She hugged her knees, her curved back as inviting to the touch as permafrost.

"Well, you know me," her tone made me want to jump out of bed and run as far away as possible, "I can't promise you anything."

The silence was an impenetrable wall between us, and a ten ton weight had descended on my heart. Then she angled her head round towards me, and I caught a flicker of something unknown in her eyes,

"What makes you think I don't think the same thing about you," she said, "with all the opportunities you get?" At the change in her voice, the ground closed up, and the weight started to lift. I don't know what sort of expression I had on my face, yet she lay down close to me again, her smile melting the block of ice encasing me. "Don't look so surprised, you're really quite attractive, you know," she murmured. Her lips grazed my neck, and I reached for her in relief.

"But I don't want to do this with anyone else," I squeaked as my erratic body decided to switch rapidly into overdrive at the touch of her hands and mouth, and our movements began to mesh.

"Neither do I." She was gasping, "So there. Mind my sports injury."

The moment of peril had passed, and we were safe.

All the same, I was in an odd mood when we left town for Wales on Tuesday, even though Liz had decided that NELS could do without her on Sunday and she would come south and join us at the weekend. Should I be reassured or not? How real was the probability that she would get bored with me, and seek some diversion in my absence? I couldn't envisage going off her unless I had a heart transplant. . .I looked out of the van window at the dull motorway and sighed.

"You're very quiet," Bill observed not unkindly, "had a bit of a domestic, have we?"

"Not really," I tried to rouse myself, "I'm not looking forward to this children's workshop business tomorrow, though."

"Don't you think it'll be fun?" His smile was nearly malicious, "Having a bunch of young admirers hanging on to your every word?"

"It'll be hell." I flinched as Dave, who was driving, abandoned at the last second an over-ambitious attempt to overtake a swaying caravan, "It's all right for you, children like you. They'll smell my fear and turn on me like piranhas."

How we had been dragooned into this workshop idea, I couldn't conceive. In addition to playing some normal, sensible gigs in south Wales, we had agreed to spend an afternoon at a youth music centre, giving laughingly entitled "masterclasses", during which we would initiate the no doubt underwhelmingly enthusiastic little darlings into the mysteries of playing folk music. The day would culminate in a dance where our pupils would play alongside us in selected numbers, and I had more than an inkling that the whole thing was going to be one of the biggest challenges of my glittering career.

The string teacher, Anne, did nothing to dispel my foreboding on our arrival at the centre after a morning of mounting nerves and inability to cope with solid food.

"What do you think of these tunes?" I asked her, as we stood waiting for our turn at the photocopier.

"Mm, mm", she looked at the sheets I'd laboriously written out in my tidiest notation. She had quite a sweet-looking face, and was very pregnant, "Probably about half of them will be able to play these, and the other half won't."

"But what am I going to do?" I wailed, "And how am I going to organise them?"

She took pity on my ineptitude and distress, "OK, don't panic. Here," she magicked some manuscript paper and a pen from a shelf, "you write out some boring long notes that the beginners can play as a sort of harmony, and I'll go and make sure they're sitting so that the marginally competent are on your right as you face them, and the others to your

68

left. You're not used to this, are you?"

"No," I began writing, "I'm terrified you won't get your money's worth from me, and the kids will riot."

She gave me a beautiful smile, "It's enough for us to mingle with the stars. They're quite well-behaved usually, just don't expect them to concentrate for too long." She plodded off, and I bent to my task.

In the event, it wasn't too dire. I managed to stop myself being sick at the practice room door, and I think it helped that I screamed and covered my ears when I asked them all to play a note so I could see if they were anything like in tune.

"Fu. . . For heaven's sake." I started to laugh, "That sounds like me after a night in the pub. Right, let's get sorted. . ."

I was genuinely astounded at how fast the afternoon went. I jumped around, making them stamp and chant my sanitised version of "Who ate all the pies" to get a rhythm, and encouraging contests to see which half of the group could play the loudest, and by the time the cacophany had brought Anne with Bill and Dave in attendance to the door, I was hoarse, exhausted and totally absorbed.

"Yes!" I punched the air when we crashed to a halt, "Play like this tonight, and even I might get up and dance for you." I was rewarded by grins and giggles.

"Teatime!" Anne delivered a stentorian bellow into the high-pitched, over-excited hubbub, "You can leave all your things here, don't push, there's plenty for everyone. . ."

The three stood aside to avoid being trampled underfoot by the stampede.

"That sounded different," Dave said. He had clearly been more restrained with his guitar group, "What tune were you meant to be playing?"

"It looks like they enjoyed it, anyway, that's the main thing." Anne touched my arm, "Come and get a cup of tea and a bun."

I realised I was ravenous. "Thank goodness. How do you cope with this all the time?"

"Zen-like detachment, ha, ha. The food's in the hall here." I decided that she was a very nice woman, especially when she shoved me into the front of the unruly queue, and bagged us places at one of those dwarfish school tables

69

which make you feel that you have swollen to twice your normal size.

"I'm afraid I won't be at the do tonight," she apologised as I ferried provisions to the table, "I get a bit tired these days. My partner should be along any minute now to pick me up."

"I think that's a wise decision." I popped a whole triangular sandwich into my mouth, "What does he do?"

"Oh. She's a she. I thought someone would have told you the scandal. . ." Did she think I'd be shocked?

"Oh right, so's mine." We both laughed. "I just assumed from, you know," I waved a hand at her bulge.

"The miracles of modern science." She looked relieved, "I thought you were, but I wasn't sure. And here she is, bang on time for a change." She turned to gaze fondly at the woman coming towards us. This time, I was shocked, and regretted having stuffed another sandwich into my jaws.

"Bel," Anne's voice was shot with love, "meet Kate, she's getting over an afternoon with my combined classes."

8

Bel recovered almost instantly, although there was no mistaking the whack of shock behind the extraordinary light blue-grey eyes which Issy used to rave about. I gave a convulsive swallow to get rid of my sandwich, and watched while she sat down next to Anne and gave her a quick all-encompassing survey.

"All right? Not too tired?" The concern in her voice sounded genuine, and she put her hand briefly on Anne's arm before looking at me, "Well, well, a blast from the past. I should have recognised your band's name when Anne told me about today. Still up north, then?" Now there wasn't the slightest hint of anything apart from a trace of ironic amusement in her words, and I saw how she and Liz must have got on like a house on fire.

"Um, yes." I knocked back some tea to try and eliminate

70

the alarming feeling that the sandwich was still lodged a few inches below my epiglottis, "You moved down here then?" There was nothing wrong with stating the obvious to cover up trauma.

"Eventually." She looked as if someone had told her a very funny joke but she couldn't laugh because she was in church, "What's the latest from the wilds of Lancashire, then?"

"Er. . ." I floundered, and was saved by Anne giving Bel's leg a resounding slap.

"Don't tell me she's another of your long line of exes," she said, obviously seeing no reason to restrain herself from giggling. "When this baby's born, we'll have to invite them all to the christening, and then I'll know I'll have no more nasty shocks."

"You'll need to book St Paul's," I said with a distinct lack of courtesy. ". . .Oops, sorry." I put my hand to my mouth.

Bel threw her head back and gave a great bark of laughter, causing various startled children to choke on their buns. "Oh my," she grinned blandly at me, "I forgot how funny you could be." She put her hand on Anne's shoulder, "No, she isn't. But she was a friend of Issy's, I told you about her."

"Oh dear," Anne said, placing her palms over her bulge, "don't start fighting in front of the infant. Shouting makes him far too lively for comfort."

"I think I need a cigarette," I scrabbled in my pockets, "I'd better go outside."

Anne gave Bel a suddenly sharp and direct glance, "You go with her, Bel. Have a little chat while I hoover up the rest of these cakes."

Bel didn't argue. "OK," she said, "back in a tick." She rose from her miniature chair, giving Anne another quick caress, and I followed her outside to a sheltered corner.

We stood in a stiff silence until I had rolled a cigarette and managed to get it alight.

"All right," all the levity had gone from Bel's voice, "how is Issy? Do you still see her?"

I exhaled the deadly, comforting smoke from my lungs, "She's . . .not bad. I've seen a bit of her recently. She has a music shop in Kirktown."

"Yeah," Bel traced a circle on the tarmac with her boot, "I

actually got in touch with Toni a few months after I left to check she was. . .all right."

"Well, she wasn't really," I saw no reason to dissemble, "she was a fucking mess." A dim realisation that months of practice with Liz had made me less inhibited dawned on me, "You were a complete shit." I forced myself to meet her penetrating gaze until her eyelids twitched in some fleeting acknowledgement.

"I know," she said, and shoved her hands in her jacket pockets with a sigh.

There was another silence.

"I don't expect you to believe me," she said, just as I was considering stubbing out my cigarette and going inside, "but I am sorry for what I did."

"Why did you do it then?" I hoped I didn't sound too angry, after all, this wasn't exactly my business, "You weren't seriously interested in Amy, were you?"

"No." Our eyes met again, and some weird current of understanding flickered between us, then disappeared. She started picking her words with care, "I thought at the time that it was only a bit of harmless fun on the side. Since then though, I've sort of realised. . .," she sighed again, "I don't expect you to believe this either, but I did love Issy. It's just that she wasn't. . .she wasn't Anne." She caught my look of confused disbelief. "I mean," she continued, "I think I wanted to finish with Issy and didn't know how to, so I did it in the cruellest and most cowardly way possible. I cheated on her and ran away, and don't think," her voice cracked a fraction, "that I haven't felt hideously guilty and upset, because I have. And I know Issy'll probably never forgive me, and why should she. Only I know I'm in love with Anne and want to stay with her and have a family, and that's what's important to me now."

"So it's turned out all right for you." I was fully aware of the contempt in my voice.

"Yes, it has. That's the way it is." This time it was me who backed down from her level stare.

I coughed, "Well, what do I know. It's all a puzzle to me. Do you mind if I tell Issy I've seen you?"

"Not at all." She gave me the beginnings of an engaging smile, "Have one of my cards to give to her, and if she wants to come after me with an axe, she can."

I tried not to smile back, "I don't think she will. By the way," I don't know what made me say this, "I'm sort of living with an old friend of yours, Liz, Liz Sharpe."

"Good Lord." Her smile broadened, "And how is she these days? Still taking photographs? Still got those lovely long legs?"

"Oh yes." Surprisingly I didn't feel even the merest twinge of jealousy, "She's coming to join us in Cardiff this weekend, if you wanted to meet up. . ."

"Aw, I can't," she replied. "We're going away for probably our last little break before the baby comes. Say hi to her for me, won't you?"

"Sure. She seems to have fond memories of you." There was a strange lightness in my heart.

Bel laughed easily, "She should have." She put one finger on my sleeve, "I think she's landed on her feet with you." She moved abruptly away, and started heading back towards the door, "Ah well, I must take Anne home."

"I hope it all goes well with the baby," I said to her back in a rush of altruism.

She stopped, and her face opened up, "Thanks. It's all gone really smoothly so far. I can't wait, actually."

She gave a little skip into the building, and I hung back for a few seconds while she returned to Anne, who was looking mildly anxious, to help her to her feet. We exchanged politely friendly goodbyes, and I went on a quest for anything left to eat and drink.

"What was all that about?" Jo asked when I joined the band at their table, a squished cake and a cup of stewed tea in my hands.

"Don't be so nosy." I caught Fred's mutter. He was the one person I knew who wasn't overfond of gossip.

"Loose ends," I said enigmatically. "What's the plot for tonight then?"

I thought my massed strings performed very creditably once they'd got over their nerves and remembered to stop waving and smirking at their relatives and friends, and a good time seemed to have been had by all. By Saturday afternoon, when we had landed up in Cardiff and I was lying on my bed for a pre-gig rest in our cheap hotel, however, I was still mulling over the peculiar meeting with Bel. Was it fate, working in some obscure way to release Issy from the ghosts of her past, or would it plunge her back into despair to hear that Bel was apparently blissfully happy in her role as expectant parent? Maybe Liz would be in a reflective mood when she arrived that night, and would give me her considered opinion. Or maybe, more likely, she would find the whole thing hilarious. There was a knock at the door.

"Go away, Bill," I shouted. "How many times do I have to tell you? You're not having my Russian navy tee shirt." He'd been making covetous noises towards this garment for days.

"I'm not Bill." The door opened, and Liz slipped inside, a lopsided smile on her face.

"Darling! You're earlier. . ." I wasn't prepared for this surging delight, and heaved myself up to get off the bed.

I saw her shoulders relax. "Don't move," she said with such amorous intensity that a shiver ran down my spine. She shut the door firmly, kicked off her boots, and lowered herself beside me. "Sweetheart, sweetheart, I found you," she murmured, her mouth searching for mine.

"How long have we got?" she breathed, her hand sliding under my shirt.

"About two hours." It could have been two minutes, wild horses wouldn't have been able to stop me.

"Thank goodness. Oh my love," she groaned out the words, her fingers on my breast, "I couldn't last till tonight. I'm dying for you to touch me."

I cried out, and we lost ourselves in the rapture of pleasing each other. I remembered, probably far too late, that the walls were very thin.

"Oh my God," she said hoarsely as our undulations slowed into receding waves, "That was incredible."

"Oh. . .oh. . .oh," I was still shuddering in the aftershock.

"We're so, so good together," she continued throatily, nuzzling my shoulder. "Well worth the drive," she added more prosaically.

I tried to bring myself back to earth. "I love you very much," I found myself saying instead, moving my head so that I could drink in every detail of her altered face. Her eyes had never been so unguarded.

"Oh angel, I'm sorry, I can't resist you. Let's do it again."

We got some very sour looks from the band when we tottered down to the hotel lobby ten minutes late.

"Never mind," Jo said kindly, "it won't take us so long to set up with Liz helping to lift and carry."

"Ha." Bill was being catty, "Neither of them could lift an eyebrow by the look of them."

Jo patted his head, "Ah, leave them alone, they're only young once." I felt suitably guilty, and smiled my gratitude at her.

Considering my somewhat atomised state, I think I played pretty well, but it turned out to be a long and noisy gig, so it was the early hours of the morning before Liz and I were able to have a sensible conversation. I told her about Bel while she tossed and turned, complaining about the lumpy bed.

"Oh right," she said, bashing at her pillow, "so she's settled down. Happens to us all. I think they've stuffed this mattress with straw. Still," she wriggled some more, "I think Issy should write to her, now you've got her address. Tell her how pissed off she was, and achieve what the Americans call closure. Which reminds me," she flailed at the covers with her legs, "Issy rang the other day. That camp at the Bradley site has got started, and we're going over there next Sunday to have a look and be supportive. The softball's on Saturday for some reason. I think you're free, are you going to come along and sing 'We shall overcome' with us?"

"Oooh, I expect so. You look like you've got St Vitus dance. D'you want to swap sides?"

She repositioned her legs, "No. You know I have to sleep on this side of you, otherwise I feel all wrong. God, this is the worst bed I've ever been in, and I've been in a few."

"Sleep on the floor, then. I'm worn out, and I'll never get any rest with you jiggling about like that." I pulled some covers my way, and tried to shut my eyes, letting my arm rest over her.

"You can't mean that. I haven't come all this way not to sleep with you." She pulled the covers back.

"You've had your wicked way, what more do you want?" I thought I would never get tired of the enticing feel of her stomach and elegant thighs. Did her comment about Bel settling down mean that she was doing the same?

"Do we have to get up for breakfast?" She had finally stopped squirming and was breathing into my ear.

"Yes," I said severely. "We've paid for it. Go to sleep."

"You're such a cruel woman. I'll get in the car and go back home."

"No you won't."

"Yes I will."

"All right, then, do, leave me in peace."

We wittered happily on until sleep overtook us.

"I thought Liz wasn't coming down till late last night," Bill said pointedly at the breakfast table the next morning. I was propping my eyes open, and Liz had gone to the kitchen door in the vain hope of finding someone to refill the teapot.

"Uuuurgh. She just decided to come a bit earlier." Speaking was nearly too much of an effort.

"I think she was checking up on you. Making sure you hadn't lured some groupie to your lair." He poked at a nasty looking lump in the sugar bowl.

"Don't be silly." I wasn't up to thinking about it, and wondered if it would be really bad manners to rest my head on the table. I'd have to sleep in the car on the way to Swansea for our next gig. Still, his words kept coming back to me over the next few days, and I was aware that I was holding back from pressing Liz on her early arrival. Things between us seemed to be running so easily, and I knew I was reluctant to rock the boat.

The next Sunday wasn't ideal for playing eco-warriors. The rain had returned in gusty showers, and I would have much preferred to spend the day in front of the fire with a book and Liz bringing me cups of tea. She was fired with determination, however, digging out my wellingtons and waving them in front of my nose so I couldn't pretend I had lost them.

"Come on, come on," she threw my old raincoat at me for good measure, "you need some fresh air."

"Why are you so keen on this?" I grumped, getting into the car. "I didn't think it would be your scene."

"All your friends will be there, and loads of other people, it'll be like a party. . .and it's years since I've been on a demo."

"This is a demo?" My voice was rising, "I thought it was just a curious visit."

"Well, maybe it's a sort of mini-rally. Just to show solidarity with the happy campers." Her eyes flashed with some hidden anticipation as she spoke, and my suspicions, never far below the surface, were aroused.

"You're expecting trouble, aren't you?" I accused her. "You want to do your action photographer thing. Don't think I haven't noticed your fancy camera, you hope there's going to be a big fight."

She laughed. "You're priceless. I only said to Eleanor that I'd be on hand to record any. . .any unprovoked hostility from the Bradley lot. They've brought in security guards, probably the same ones who chased Ag."

"Oh God." I lapsed into silence as we swished through the damp lanes, and tried to appreciate the welcome flush of green springing along the copses and hedges.

It was clear that the inclement weather hadn't deterred BAG supporters from turning out in force, and we had to park a fair way from the site at the end of a straggling line of scruffy cars and camper vans plastered with old CND stickers. I felt the stirrings of a reluctant excitement. After all, I moaned enough about the loss of the countryside to greedy developers, so perhaps it was time I did something positive, however minute, and the steady, comforting feel of Liz's hand in mine, allied with a break in the clouds, perked me up some more.

"You should have brought your fiddle," she said, smiling down at me, "given us a rousing tune."

I smiled back, "Maybe the next time. I could stand in front of the diggers, playing a lament. That would make a nice photo for your portfolio."

"Yeah, it could go next to that one of you serenading me with nothing on. The one that's going to have pride of place when I hold my exhibition in the main art gallery." Her thumb caressed my palm.

"You dare, that was meant for your private enjoyment only." I never took this threat very seriously, believing that even she would balk at posting up my naked image for all to see.

"Great art should be shared," she replied sententiously.

"And a great bum," she added, bursting into gales of laughter.

Snorting and snuffling, we arrived at the camp. It lay on a broad strip of field between a line of woods and what was evidently the Bradley site, and looked like a manic cross between a scout jamboree and the encampment of some multi-ethnic army from the Middle Ages. Clustered around a brown marquee was a scattering of modern tents and a motley collection of makeshift benders, domes and yurts, decorated with scraps of bunting, bright flags snapping in the wind and wet clothes. Woodsmoke billowed from smouldering fires, and a snaking line of people blobbed along a wire fence dividing the building site from the camp, tying ribbons and placards to its strands. Not that there seemed to be much building going on today. On the other side of the fence, a solitary digger crouched motionless at the end of the deep scar made by its tracks, and a few burly figures in fluorescent waistcoats drifted in and out of the couple of portakabins rising up from the churned grass. The gateway to the camp was adorned with a huge banner proclaiming that this was the Bradley Action Group Monitoring Station, with an admonishing sign shouting "Absolutely no vehicles whatsoever beyond this point!" A table, protected by an ingenious canvas awning, stood just inside the gateway, and there, heads together over piles of paper and nattering like two stallholders at a village bazaar, were Issy and Eleanor.

"Just the person!" Eleanor grinned up at Liz after our shouted greetings, "I've got a little job for you. Got your camera? Yes? Right," she was all brisk efficiency, "our main tactic here is to niggle away at the builders to make sure that they don't move an inch over the site boundary or damage anything they're not meant to. See that copse?" She pointed at a bunch of trees on the far side of the site, "They're not meant to touch those. So what I thought, Liz, was that you could maybe walk round the site with me and take a load of photos to show what it's like now, before they've really got started. And if you could come back every now and then, we'd have a record of before and after, and what they're up to."

"Fine by me," Liz was being remarkably malleable, "I can

leave our number with the people here as well, so they can ring me if they hear chainsaws in that wood, and I'll be down to snap them red-handed."

"Brilliant." Eleanor picked up a bundle of large-scale maps, "Shall we get started? I'm afraid we can't pay you the going rate, but we can probably scrape up some money for film and developing from our fighting fund." She stood up, "We're arranging a benefit concert night, and Issy's band are going to come down for their debut performance."

Her enthusiasm was infectious. "When will it be?" I asked rashly, "I could see if we're free, and twist our lot's arm into putting in an appearance."

"Would you?" Eleanor's eyes lit up even more, "We haven't decided on a date, and I'll understand if you're busy, but if you could make it, it would be. . .tremendous."

"Be careful," Issy warned, her mouth twitching, "you're in danger of becoming a right on couple. Why don't you sit here with me, Kate, and keep me company while they do their surveillance act. There's an urn in the marquee, we can have some tea and scandalise."

"Goody, goody." I sat down on the deck chair vacated by Eleanor, "Where's Tam?"

"With Jeanie and Alison, I hope." She glanced vaguely around, "They're about somewhere, getting up to no good, I expect."

We watched Liz and Eleanor walk purposefully off, and I wondered if I should remark yet again on Amy's absence. Something told me as well that this was not a good time to tell Issy about Bel.

"Amy's working again," Issy said as if she had read my thoughts, "she's in Preston for the weekend."

"Oh." I raised my eyebrows, "What's the latest with those two?"

"Er." She made a dodgy gesture with her hand, "A bit delicate, I think. How about that tea?"

I took the hint, and went to the marquee to find sustenance.

Issy and I sat at our post, handing out flyers, explaining what was going on to new arrivals, and enduring another vicious rain squall until Liz and Eleanor returned, looking pleased with themselves.

"I'll develop these tomorrow," Liz was saying, "and give you copies, and keep the negatives in a safe place."

"You're a total asset." Eleanor put the damp maps back on the table and looked at her watch, "A reporter from the local rag is due at two, so I'll start rounding up the rest of the steering group for interviews. I'll see if I can find someone to replace you Iss, so you can have a mingle, instead of being stuck here." She whizzed off, as fast as the mud would allow.

"Doesn't she ever stop?" Liz asked, perching on the edge of the table and squinting aimlessly through a lens at the portakabins, "I'm quite worn out.

Fucking hell!" She sprang up as if she had sat on a drawing pin, gave an enraged bellow, and with a wild gesture at a man who had come out of one of the cabins to use his mobile phone, promptly destroyed the respectable image she had built up with my friends. "It's that bastard cheating bootlegger Jock!"

9

"What?" I jumped out of my chair, as Liz danced up and down on the spot.

"There!" She pointed again, let rip with a piercing "Oi!" and set off sprinting towards the fence. I gave chase, leaving Issy open-mouthed behind us, only to see the man look up at the commotion, take the phone from his ear, and scuttle hastily behind the portakabin. There was the roar of an engine, a slurpy grinding of mud and stones under wheels, and I caught the rear end of a previously concealed car careering over ruts and puddles towards the site exit.

"Bastard!" Liz repeated, coming to a halt at the fence and kicking at a tussock of grass, "Fucking bastard!"

"Are you sure it was him?" I wheezed, the breath heaving in and out of my chest as I came level with her.

"Of course I am," she snarled, "I saw him clear as day in

my telephoto lens."

"Well, what's he doing here? I thought he'd been arrested."
My heart was beginning a downward journey to the soles of
my old wellies at the prospect of this particular can of worms
being reopened.

"How the fuck should I know?" she shouted. So much for
our stab at being the perfect couple, "He probably got off,
the git. Right," she put her hand on a fence post, "I'm going
to get to the bottom of this." She lifted her head and yelled
at the top of her voice, "Hey, come out here someone! I want
to talk!"

One of the portakabin doors swung open, and a figure
swaggered out to the accompaniment of a burst of coarse
male laughter. He was a stupid-looking, superficially
handsome young man, and he thrust his way slowly towards
us, thumbs hooked into the waistband of his jeans.

"Yeah?" he drawled, as if he had seen too many tough guy
movies.

"Hey, mate," Liz said in a not unfriendly manner, "can you
tell me who that man was with the mobile phone and what
he's doing here?"

He looked us up and down with the disturbing assurance
of a bully who knows his older brothers will kick the shit out
of anyone who dares to stand up to him.

"Piss off, filthy fucking dykes," he said.

It took me a while to register what he had said, and that
he wasn't joking, and when I did, I felt as if I had been
physically assaulted. All the confidence gained from years of
affection and acceptance swirled away down some inner
plughole, and I was back to being a confused, unhappy and
lonely thirteen year old. I felt my face go white, and I half-
turned away to shrivel to a shameful knot inside my raincoat.
I was still able to sense Liz's rage beside me, and for a mad
moment thought she was going to vault the fence and punch
him in his ignorant face. Instead, she raised her camera
slowly and deliberately, and took a rapid succession of
photos. He backed away a step.

"I'll know you again," Liz said in a calm voice I had never
heard before.

Somewhere, he was frightened as well. "Fuck off," he said
loudly, and started walking away.

"Come on." Liz put her hand on my sleeve, "We're not going to get any sense out of that wanker." Then she saw my face. "Jesus, Kate," she put her precious camera on the wet ground and wrapped me in her arms, "Babe, it's all right, he's not going to hurt you."

"I'm sorry," I sobbed against her, hot tears coursing down my cheeks, "I'm sorry. . ."

"Ssh, it's ok," she spoke into my hair, "it's ok, you're all right."

Now not sure of exactly why I was crying, I bawled on, ending in a great shuddering sigh. I leaned into her, and, for a second, felt an extraordinary sensation of complete safety emanating from her bones, before I pulled away and wiped my eyes on my sleeve.

"I'm sorry, I don't know what came over me," I sniffed.

"Here," Liz produced a crumpled tissue, "I don't think I've used this one. Don't be sorry," she touched my damp face, "you're not used to stuff like that, are you?"

"No." I blew my nose, "You must think I'm really wet."

She put her arms back round me, and gave me a bear-like hug. "No I don't," she said. She lowered her voice, "Don't ever be ashamed of us," she whispered almost savagely, then she released me and started walking towards the marquee. "Let's get a cup of tea," she said in her normal voice, "I'm gasping."

Issy had disappeared, and, still a bit shaken, I huddled on a straw bale in the fuggy marquee, only vaguely aware of the other clumping figures smelling of smoke and unwashed garments, while Liz went to chat up the straggly-haired woman standing guard over a blackened metal container balanced precariously on a gas ring. My mind was whirling like an out of control film projector. What was the meaning of Jock's reappearance, of my over-reaction to a bit of abuse, of Liz's sudden and un-looked for protectiveness? Oh hell, I was going to cry again, and here Liz was, coming back. I struggled to compose myself, and to take hold of the non too clean mug she was proferring me without dropping it. She sat down next to me, and dug in her pocket.

"There you are," she said, extracting something wrapped in a scrap of kitchen roll, "special cake. Have a bite now, to cheer you up, and we can share the rest tonight." She winked extravagantly.

I was touched, sometimes she could be illogically puritanical about drugs. "Where did you get this?" I gawped, taking a discreet nibble or two of the pungent brownie.

"My underworld connections," she hissed out of the corner of her mouth. "We won't tell Eleanor. Put it away now, or you'll be all over the shop in an hour. Do you want to hear my theory?" she continued, as I stowed the parcel in the inside pocket of my raincoat.

"All righty," I said, snuggling closer to her, wondering if enjoying being looked after like this was a sign of gross emotional immaturity.

"Well, obviously, Jock either escaped being arrested or hasn't been charged or is on bail or something like that. I don't think he's an engineer or a builder, so I'm wondering if he's connected with those security arseholes. I wouldn't be surprised if it's his firm. It's just the kind of thing a prick like him would be involved in."

"Mm," I drank some tea, feeling warm and sleepy all of a sudden.

"And if you think about it," she rumbled on, "if he wasn't there at Kerrbank Mains that night, the police might not have got on to him at all. If all the drivers just knew him as Jock, and if he hired a lockup there under a false name or through a middleman. . .he could be the elusive Mr Big of the Borders crime scene. Are you dozing off there?"

"No." I rubbed my eyes, "What are you going to do about this?"

"Oooh," she gave me a sly smile, "I could just move into the camp here and lurk in wait for him until he turns up again. Then I'll set Oscar on him, or ambush him with a bunch of these hairy men and threaten to break his legs 'till he hands over my money. Or," she screwed up her face as if she was sucking on a piece of lemon, "I could tell Eleanor everything. It might be useful for her to know that Bradley's are employing a villain."

I woke up. "But that'll mean telling Eleanor about your spot of van driving. She'd have to go to the police if she wanted to land Bradley's in it."

"I know." She was going ever so slightly red, "Difficult, hey? Maybe she can get me diplomatic immunity or whatever it's called."

I stared at her oddly shame-faced expression, "I don't want you to be arrested and sent to prison," I blurted out.

She laughed. "I won't be, you ninny. I'll just think about having a word with El, that's all. Although you'll come and visit me in the nick, won't you? Oh look, there's Ag luring some poor unsuspecting male into her clutches."

I focussed my eyes on the middle distance, and watched Ag fluttering her eyelids at a grubby but very good-looking young man. She saw me, and shot us a "Don't you dare come and talk to me" glare.

"Cooee," Liz shouted and waved anyway, "come and introduce us to your nice friend."

Ag gave us the finger, and we spent the next hour or so chatting with people we knew and catching up on the gossip.

We were on the verge of leaving and going home to light the fire and indulge ourselves with the cake, and, I secretly hoped, the bottle of expensive massage oil I'd splashed out on a few days before, when we were accosted by Eleanor and Issy, together with Jeanie, Alison and Tam, the latter three having spent most of the afternoon in a barn, judging by the wisps of hay clinging to their coats and hair.

"Hey, you two," Eleanor smiled sweetly at us, "can you do us a favour?"

"Does it involve being outside?" I asked, peering out of the marquee at the rain which was lashing down in stair rods again.

"Not really," Eleanor replied, "but my car's buggered. Jeanie says she can fix it if she can get the part, so could you give me and her and Issy a lift to the Lodge Hotel where Issy's van is parked? Then Jeanie can go off in it and blag a part off one of her mechanic friends in town, and we could have a cream tea while we wait for her. My treat, we want a break from here. Or," she must have noticed the lustful glint in my eyes, "you could just drop us off and go home."

"I met up with El in the Lodge car park," Issy explained, "and drove down here with her in her car. So we looked more environmental." The Lodge was a hideous, but handily placed, modern construction on the edge of town near the motorway exit.

"And I'll stay here with Tam," Alison announced, trying to

look virtuous, "till they come back in the van."

"No problem," Liz declared, "Kate has never knowingly refused free food. We should all be able to squeeze in." And my shouting and swearing earlier was totally out of character, she might as well have added.

I had been weighing up the rival attractions of a guaranteed cream tea I didn't have to pay for and of the possibility of exotic practices with Liz, and had come to the conclusion that I could have them both if I played my cards right.

"Will they let me in the Lodge like this?" I demurred, looking down at my wellingtons.

"You could lose the coat," Liz said practically, "and I think I saw your baseball boots in the car. You don't look too disgusting." I stuck my tongue out at her, and we raced through the wet to the car.

Liz and I started arguing almost as soon as Issy and Eleanor had settled into the back seat with Jeanie jammed between them, and Liz began to attempt a three point turn in the narrow lane.

"Why are you turning round?" I needled provocatively.

"What?" She spun the wheel and inched forwards, "Because this is the way back to town." She frowned in her effort to avoid swiping the car in front.

"Well, yes," I undid the buttons of my dripping coat and started to ease it off, succumbing to the temptation of a mindless fight, "but it would be quicker to go straight on and go on the motorway if we're going to the Lodge. . ..Stop! You're too close."

"For God's sake," Liz braked dramatically, "who's driving this car? It's no quicker by the motorway."

"Yes it is," I said automatically. "You just don't want to admit you don't know the way, and you don't want to take directions from me."

She swore terribly. "I take enough directions from you, so shut up."

She reversed a bit too far, and there was a nasty jolt and downwards jerk as one of the rear wheels went into a ditch. "Now look what you've made me do!" she yelled.

"You did it all yourself," I swatted back, and turned to the three behind us, "can any of you see a pair of baseball boots?"

"Fuck your boots!" Liz hit the steering wheel, "You drive me nuts!"

Issy and Eleanor had their hands over their mouths, while Jeanie looked like a shocked owl on her perch.

"Do you always carry on like this?" she asked in disbelief.

"Tss," I heard Issy whisper, "this is just their idea of foreplay."

"Hell," Jeanie didn't bother to lower her voice, "they're not going to have sex now, are they?"

"Probably. And then they'll end up in traction." Eleanor's words sounded muffled.

"Right!" Liz unclenched her hands from the wheel, leaned over me, grabbed my head and gave me a ferocious snog.

"Oh, oh Kate," she simpered, releasing me a fraction, "I could drown in your eyes."

"Darling! Take me now!" I cried, starting to giggle uncontrollably. I'd had a few more bites of the cake when she wasn't looking.

"Aw God," Issy and Eleanor groaned simultaneously, and Jeanie covered her eyes while my hysterics ran their course.

Somehow we managed to push the car out of the ditch, and to arrive at the Lodge, by Liz's route, all in one piece.

"Give us your van keys, Issy," Jeanie said wearily as we decanted from the car, "I'm getting away from you lunatics. See you back here when I've got the part."

I realised I was still wearing my wellingtons. "Oops, must change my shoes," I trilled, and swayed back to the car, collapsing on the front seat. My knees felt very peculiar. I flung off the wellies and tried to put on the canvas boots I'd finally found in the boot.

Liz gave me a suspicious look. "Hang on," she said to the others, and draped herself over my legs to pick up my coat from the floor. She felt in the pocket. "I thought so," she said, putting her finger under my chin, "I can't take you anywhere."

"You can have the rest," I said cheerfully, tugging at my boots.

"What rest?" She put the coat on the back seat, and resumed her study of my face, "Are you going to disgrace me in there?"

"No. You have a lovely mouth," I said inconsequentially.

Her lovely mouth relaxed. "This should be fun." She looked at my feet, "Can you tie your laces yourself?"

"Of course." I gave one of the laces a vigorous pull, and it promptly snapped. "Dearie me," I remarked, "got any string on you?"

Her body started to quiver. "You're such a bad influence," she said, pretty unfairly I thought. "Come on, the others are waiting."

Foolishly, the hotel staff let us in, and agreed to serve us.

"It's not a very nice place," Eleanor said sotto voce as we flopped around a table in the lounge area, "but the cream teas are spot on."

"I think I came here with Chloe once," I tried to sound normal, "for a university do, when I was being a lecturer's spouse. I fell in the swimming pool and we had to leave. Chloe was furious, she made me sleep in the spare room for a week. I suffered with that woman, I bet I never told you the half of it." I looked up, "What's so funny?"

"I'd forgotten what you were like when you're stoned," Eleanor said, "you've been at those naughty cakes they were making earlier, haven't you? Just remember I don't know anything about them."

"Ee," I had turned into my granny, "you have to be up early in the morning to get one past you."

"She'll be all right when the food comes," Liz's voice wafted up from the depths of her armchair, "at least it'll stop her talking."

Eleanor was right, the tea was more than adequate, and the effects of the cake wore off slightly as I steadily ploughed my way through a tumulus of scones and a bathful of cream.

"El," Liz said when all that was left was a pile of crumbs and I was on my fourth cup of tea, "can I have a little word with you at another table?" I hadn't been beyond noticing her internal struggle as we ate. So, she was going to confess, the noble thing.

"Sure, let's go over there," Eleanor stood up obligingly, and the two of them moved to a table in the window.

I settled back, and watched Liz start a stumbling conversation, her forehead resting on her hand and her feet nervously twisting round her chair legs. She had to be the most attractive woman I had ever seen. What was it, I started an intellectual conversation with myself, that made me want her so much practically all the time? A mere chemical reaction, a neurotic fixation coming from arrested development, or was it a cosmic meeting of souls? I sniggered at this last thought, and brought myself back to speak to Issy. It didn't take me long to realise that her gaze was as fixed on Eleanor as mine had been on Liz. Shit, I thought, what's going on here? I must have made some surprised grunt, because Issy blinked and smiled uncertainly at me.

"What?" she said vaguely.

"Er, nothing," I mumbled. "Where do you think Jeanie is? She's missed all the food."

"Oh, she's in love. She'll be drivelling on about Alison to her mechanic friends. What did Liz want to talk to Eleanor about, if you don't mind me asking? Is it about that man she saw?"

"Yes, she's confessing her sins," I said darkly. "She may have some dirt on that security firm Bradleys have at the site."

"Oh good," she said, her mind obviously still miles away. Now or never, I told myself.

"Issy," I started, "I have to tell you this. I saw Bel when I was in Wales last week. She turned up at some workshop we were doing."

"Who?" she said abstractedly.

"Issy! Bel, you know, the woman who broke your heart." I never said tact was my middle name.

"Oh that Bel." She hit her forehead, "Silly me. So how is she?"

Taken aback by her reaction, I told her everything, and it began to sink in.

"Ah well," she said sadly when I'd finished, "at least I know now that she wasn't totally indifferent to me."

"I've got her address," I said, "will you write to her?"

"Maybe. If I ever get my head sorted out. . ." her voice tailed away, and she raised her eyes to stare thoughtfully at a group of men in suits who were congregating at the other end of the lounge. "Where've I seen that man before?" she muttered. ". . .Ah, I know, he works for Boltons. He came in the shop to speak to me about money for the band. . .I'm sorry, Kate," she ran her hands through her hair, "thanks for telling me all this. I just don't know how I feel any more. It's all a bit weird. . ." She stopped as Eleanor and Liz, who was looking very pleased with herself, came back to our table.

"Got the opposition in as well, I see," Eleanor pronounced, flicking her eyes towards the businessmen, "that's Bradley's legal team and some other management farts. Having a crisis meeting I hope."

"Including a guy who works for Boltons," Issy said, her face searching Eleanor's.

"Oh my," Eleanor bared her teeth in her unprofessionally evil smile, "the plot is thickening. Jeanie was right, you know, Boltons and Bradleys are all part of the same group, and there are rumours going round that Boltons are in financial trouble. Something iffy is definitely going on here, I'm going to do some more digging."

Issy gave an involuntary start. "You'll be careful, won't you?" she said, and then went pink and shut her mouth.

"Of course." Eleanor appeared unconcerned, "It's only a game really. But a fascinating one." She smiled at me, "Feeling a little more with us now, are we?"

"I think so." I grinned back, "A bit full, actually. Thanks for the tea."

"You're welcome, thanks for the lift," she replied. "And thanks, Liz, I'm glad you told me what you did. It all helps, and you can trust me." She turned to Issy, "Where's your girlie, then? I want to get going. . ."

"What did Eleanor say?" I asked Liz as she drove us home.

"She was very, very interested," Liz had her complacent look on, "and she assures me she can keep me out of jail."

I yawned, "That's a relief." I made an executive decision to stop puzzling about the disturbing connections between Boltons, Bradleys and Jock, and to think massage oil instead. When I'd lit the fire, however, I lay down for a few minutes on the settee to plan my campaign, and the next thing I knew was Liz standing over me with a pint glass of water in her hand.

"I saw you regaining consciousness," she said, "I thought you might like this."

"Shankth." I drank as if I had been in the desert for weeks. The room looked different. "You've tidied up," I squawked, "I didn't hear you."

"I'm not surprised," she moved my legs slightly and sat down, "you were in a coma. You dreadful addict," her warm tone belied her words, "I should never have put temptation in your path. Would you like some tea as well?"

"Mm." The room was very quiet, and I heard the minute tinkle of coal in the grate and the reassuring tide of her breath. "Why are you so nice to me?" The question popped out of my mouth before I could censor it.

Her lips parted, "Oh Kate, you're so easy to please. A few scraps of food, the odd cup of tea and," she bent towards me, "The odd bit of this. . ."

"I'm glad you closed the curtains," I said after a while, "it would spoil this if the neighbours were watching."

10

The stand-off between BAG and the developers continued over the next few weeks. Liz reported that although the security men were still milling around the place, no sighting of Jock had been mentioned, no actual work had started and Eleanor, citing all sorts of obscure precedents and legal obfuscations, was gleefully blocking the District Council's attempt to clear the camp off the field. The benefit concert was fixed for a Friday in May, and, due to a cancellation arising from a black hole in the finances of a student union, it looked as if the band would be able to play after all.

"The BAG organisers want us to do the closing set," Fred announced when he'd broken the sad news that we wouldn't be getting a lot of money for entertaining a crowd of smashed students at a May Ball, "and I know we won't get paid, but it's all good publicity, and at least the punters might be better behaved, and our lives and equipment won't be in danger."

"Besides which," Jo added, "it means we won't have to travel back for that posh wedding party we're doing on the Saturday night. We can all look clean and smart, instead of ravaged and worn out."

We all knew that we had only been asked to play for this reception, at a country house just over the county border in Yorkshire, because the bride's father, a self-made millionaire, wanted to go one up on his neighbour who had hired a chamber orchestra for a similar do, by having a band which would make more noise. Since we were charging a big fat fee, we didn't mind, and, instead of relying on luck or whoever might be supplied by the venue, were planning to take along one of Bill's friends to work the sound deck and ensure that we were playing at full volume. I disliked the whole hassle that went with being amplified and, unlike Dave, had never fully mastered the intricacies of wiring and microphones, but I was willing to go along with the others for a bit of fun. Deep in our hearts, we all nursed a secret ambition for the police to order us to turn it down.

"It's a shame I won't be here for the benefit. Especially now you're playing, and Issy's band as well."

Liz's over the shoulder remark caught me by surprise. We were spending a rare afternoon together being domesticated, which meant that we were making a half-hearted effort to clear a back log of dirty clothes and pots.

"What? Why not?" I said sharply, dropping the bulging wet quilt cover which had swallowed up all the other washing in the machine.

"Don't you ever look at that calendar?" Liz flicked a handful of suds at me from the sink, "I'm going to Bath for my mum's retirement party. I've told you about a hundred times."

"Oh." I started pulling tangled socks out of the cover, "I didn't realise it was that particular Friday."

"Well it is." She carried on scrubbing at a pan in which I'd tried to boil potatoes without any water, and we continued in silence for a while.

"Oh don't sulk," she said eventually, "I'm only going for the Friday night, and since you can't come with me, you can hardly complain."

"I know, I know." I sighed in a martyred fashion, picked up the washing basket and headed for the line in our back yard.

She gave me a look, and then noticed the washing. "Ah Kate, you haven't," she said.

"Haven't what?" I tried to cover the basket with my arm.

"Put that red shirt in again. Jeez, how many times. . ." I could tell that through some miracle she wasn't properly annoyed.

"I thought you liked pink underwear," I said, and put the basket down so she could chase me round the house.

It was true that I had managed to forget exactly when she was going to Bath for her family shindig. I had never met her mother, although I had spoken to her on the phone, and had always been disconcerted by this disembodied replica of Liz's voice enquiring after my health and travels with the band. The relationship between the two of them was something Liz rarely commented upon, but even I had worked out that it was very different from the amiable bond, based on the unspoken mutual agreement that we would never understand each other, that existed between me and my parents. Liz's phone conversations with her usually took the form either of character assassinations of people in Bath or of furious fights, with both of them dredging up over thirty years' worth of failures and shortcomings and struggling to get the last insult in before the other person slammed the receiver down. Liz was always unfazed by these interactions.

"We like annoying each other," was all she would say, "we've always been like this." Although, like me, she wasn't the precise model of a devoted daughter, I was aware that she had set her heart on putting in an appearance at this party, and, I was belatedly realising, would have liked me to come as well. After all, she had done her duty and met my parents when we fitted in a flying visit between Christmas and New Year, and had so thoroughly charmed them that even my mother's expression of faint alarm that I had attracted such an exotic creature had worn off by the time we left. Still, she wouldn't ask me directly to abandon the band to go south with her, so I didn't offer, even though I guessed that since it was a benefit, the others wouldn't have been too miffed if I'd said I couldn't make it.

There was a lot that wasn't being said between us in the weeks leading up to the benefit. On the surface, we carried on as we always did. I went away and came back, Liz took photos, taught her classes and played softball, and we argued and spent as much time as we could in bed.

Something was going on with Liz, though, that I didn't understand. It wasn't that she was more moody or withdrawn, in fact, she was uncharacteristically mellow and thoughtful, and this had me worried, especially since she had added a new look to her repertoire of amused, shifty, coldly detached, angry and desirous. I found her giving it me one evening as I was singing to myself while I was putting a new string on my violin, and I thought she was reading the local paper. I happened to look up and see the curious puzzled slant in her eyes before she quickly bent her head back to the page. I didn't say anything. I thought I knew her well enough to sense that she wasn't feeling guilty about anything, such as carrying on with someone else behind my back, to take a random example. Guilt usually rendered her arctically remote, and not the faintest whiff of anything untoward in her activities during my absences had reached my ears from my usual sources, nor had her ardour diminished. That was another thing. She had never been less than the most generous of lovers, but now, even more than ever, she treated me with a delicate consideration that I found both unbelievably erotic and almost unbearably moving, and which frequently left me fighting back tears. I couldn't fool myself that I wasn't deeply in love with her, yet I couldn't get a handle on what it was that wasn't quite right between us. It wasn't like it had been with Chloe, when I saw something which I'd always assumed to be solid and permanent crumbling away like a sandcastle under an incoming tide of faithlessness and lies, nor was it like the awkwardness arising from a regretted fling. It was more as if we were both standing on the bank of a river which we would probably have to cross, and into which neither of us was willing to dip the first toe.

I was musing over all this while I sat with Jo in a greasy spoon somewhere in the Midlands on the Saturday before the benefit. We had left the men doing something technical in the hall we were playing that night, and I had just had an affectionate and joky conversation with Liz on the phone.

"You all right, Kate?" Jo asked suddenly.

I broke off my contemplation of a crusty ketchup bottle. "Yeah, fine," I replied.

She didn't look convinced, but didn't say anything else

right away. We had always rubbed along pretty well together, although I found her a much more private person than Pat, her sister-in-law and my former landlady, whom I treated like a second mother. Sometimes when our performances together took off beyond the everyday, I felt an intense closeness with her, almost as intimate as if we were making love, and we seemed to balance that by keeping a definite distance from each other in the hurly burly of normal life. This time, however, she advanced cautiously over the usual space between us.

"Tell me to shut up if you want," she said, "but can I ask, are you feeling a bit under pressure at the moment? You know, trying to fit in the band and Liz and everything?"

I nodded, and covered my eyes as I started to cry. "Hell," I said, "I'm sorry, I'm sure I never used to do all this weeping before I met Liz."

"I don't know." I could sense her smile, "You did a good impression of a waterfall when you were splitting up with Chloe." She leaned back in her chair, "Here we all were, thinking you'd found true love at last, and that we wouldn't have to spend the band's profits on kleenex any more. How could we have been so wrong? Is it that bad?"

I sniffed a bit, then it all came out in a rush. "I'm just so confused and torn," I babbled, "I really really love the band, it's my life, and I really really love Liz and I couldn't stand losing her, and it's all right when we're just away for weekends or a few days, but I don't know what'll happen when we go on this tour, and what about next year if we go on this trip to the States? I can hardly pop back in between gigs to check she hasn't run off with someone else, can I? It's a mess, my whole life's a mess," I concluded woefully. The proposed tour of the States, which Fred had only recently sprung on us, was like a last straw.

"Hm," she looked gravely at me, "I can see it's not easy. I mean, it's been all right so far, hasn't it? We're not a top band, we haven't done massive tours, we just nip here and there in the winter, do the festivals in the summer and always come home in between. And that's fitted in with Dave's teaching, and me and Fred doing our stuff with other bands. Oh God," she started retying her ponytail, "going to the States would be such a break for us, though. It could be a last chance for Fred and me to really do something. We're good enough, you know, and," her gaze on me was more than usually piercing, "you're good enough too. But," she rested her hands on the table and took a deep breath, "I'm not being cruel here, Kate, you must know we all think the world of you, you're one of us and it would be awful not to have you with us. Still, if we decide to go, we need. . .we need your commitment." She groaned, "Er, I'm not much good at this, what I think I'm trying to say is that we'd understand if you decided your heart wasn't in the States thing, and that you'd rather stay with Liz."

I was stunned. "Are you planning to replace me?" I whispered, feeling as pole-axed as if my parents had told me I was adopted.

"No, you silly thing!" I couldn't remember seeing Jo lose her cool like this before, "We all just want you to be happy! If you'd be happier with Liz than with us, then we'll have to put up with it, and find someone else to entertain us with their rich and varied love life."

I was quiet for a while.

"The problem is," I ventured, "what if I leave the band and it doesn't work out between Liz and me? She might go off me, maybe it just works now because we aren't together all the time, my heart would be broken, I'd lose everything and," I had another thought, "I'd have to get a job."

"Waaa!" Jo gripped the table, "Have a little optimism, for God's sake. I give up," she began to laugh, "has it never occurred to you that Liz might love you as much as you love her, that loads of bands would like you to join them and that you were really good with those children and could get into teaching if you wanted to settle down?"

"No," I replied. I didn't believe a word of what she'd just said.

"I give up," she repeated and stood up, "come on, let's go and see what the boys are up to. One thing though," she turned serious again as we left the cafe, "my advice, for what it's worth, is that you should tell Liz the truth. Tell her what you said to me, try and have a proper talk with her about where you're both going. Then at least you'll know where you stand. And cheer up, we'll let you play a nice long fast solo tonight, just to take your mind off your problems."

Reassured by the fact that the rest of the band, once we

joined them, treated me no differently from normal, I let absorption in our playing do its customary magic of taking me far away from my bothersome emotions, and I put my tortuous mind processes on a temporary hold.

I didn't forget what Jo had said, however, and when I arrived home early on Sunday evening, I had resolved to grasp the nettle, stop beating about the bush, take the bull by the horns and have a serious heart to heart with Liz. I strode through the door, put down my fiddle case and bags, and heard her voice from the bathroom.

"Kate, Kate, you're back! Come up, my little honey bun."

Don't weaken, I warned sternly, and ran up the stairs. She was reclining in the bath wearing a broad grin, her wet hair sleek on her head.

"We won, we won," she crowed, "we won the softball. Come and help me celebrate." She held out her arms.

I crouched by the side of the bath, "Liz, I've been thinking, we need to. . .," my mouth went unbidden to her beautiful shoulders.

"Need to do this," she tugged at my sweatshirt with soapy hands, "God, you're gorgeous, quick, please. . ."

My treacherous anatomy gave in and I came to the conclusion that maybe I needn't say anything for a while.

"I went to Toni's last night for supper like I said," Liz said later as I leaned against the kitchen door jamb watching her cook, "Eleanor and Amy were there." Her deft hands bent spaghetti into a bubbling pan, "How hungry are you?"

"Very. How was it?" I said, deciding that her ears were the best I'd ever seen.

"Well, you know, a bit strained. Catch," she tossed a lettuce at me, "tear that up, would you sweetie? Eleanor and Amy were making an effort but I think they're on the rocks." She gave me her shifty look, "Amy and Toni talked about people I didn't know and I'm afraid I got a bit bored of legal discussions with El, so I livened things up by telling them about the time you raped me in France."

"Liz!" I screeched, spraying lettuce leaves everywhere, "you didn't! How could you, they'll all think I'm perverted. And anyway," I hit her upper arm with less force than she deserved, "it wasn't rape, you enjoyed it."

"I know," she grinned and put her arms round my waist,

96

"but I think your friends should get the chance to know the truth about you and your terrible temper. By the way," she rested her feet on mine to stop me kicking her shins, "what's that bottle of massage oil doing hiding in the food cupboard?"

I wanted to lie her down and pour it slowly over every inch of her body. "I'm going to poison your salad with it, to pay you back for your lies," I said. "Your pan's boiling over. What legal discussions were you having with Eleanor?"

"Oh, nothing really." She let me go and turned the hotplate down, "Business stuff. What's going on with her and Issy then?"

And I thought I was the only one to notice. "So you saw as well," I said, "I thought it was my imagination. I think Issy's keen on her."

"Yeah," she stirred her sauce pan and licked the wooden spoon, "wow, I'm such a good cook. They should stop farting around and just do it. I can't think why Eleanor and Amy are doing this we must stick together routine when they don't fancy each other any more. I wouldn't. Haven't you done that salad yet?"

"Um, not quite." I tried not to feel the contraction in my heart, "Where've you put the sharp knife?"

We never had our serious talk, and Liz left on Friday morning before I'd managed to get up.

"What time are you setting off for that reception thing tomorrow evening?" she asked, sitting on the bed, her leather jacket already on.

"About six." I stretched my arm out to stroke her hand.

"I'll be well back by then." Her fingers caressed mine, "My plan is to get there early so I can help them set the party up, but to leave first thing tomorrow so I get out of clearing up and," her eyes were steady on my face, "catch you before you go."

Our kiss was long and tender. Some stupid stubbornness stopped me from leaping out of bed shouting that I was going with her. I had plenty of opportunity over the next forty eight hours to curse my ridiculous pride.

11

The weekend started promisingly enough. I slopped around in my usual manner for most of Friday, and then met up with Toni at the run down hall where the benefit was being held. The rest of the band, with all our stuff, weren't arriving till later, but I had no intention of missing Issy's lot, who were opening the proceedings.

"You've got to sit with me, Kate," Toni looked more like a worriedly conspiratorial teenager than a respectable academic, "Amy's coming with Eleanor, and I don't want to be stuck between those two and Issy."

"Oo-er," I said, sipping my abstemious lemonade, "is it an official flirtation between Issy and El then?"

"No!" Toni hushed me, "You mustn't say a word. I mean, they've been seeing quite a bit of each other, but they're just friends. It's only that I don't think Eleanor has exactly told Amy how matey she and Issy are nowadays."

"Right," I said, "I'll make mindless conversation and I won't mention the war."

I saw what Liz had meant when Eleanor and Amy joined us not long after. I was shocked by the change in Amy, and it wouldn't have taken the most sensitive of souls to sense the disgruntled narkiness creeping just below the surface of their attempts at sociability. I had always remembered Amy as being plump and cheerful, yet now she appeared flabby rather than comfortably rounded, and there were new disapproving lines around her mouth. Although I tried to fight it, I knew they were doing what Chloe and I had done, playing the happy couple, when really someone should have told them to stop pretending. Since I wasn't quite up to that role, I drivelled away about the band, the house Liz and I were renting, Liz's prowess at softball and anything else I could dredge up, and was hugely relieved when a crash of drums outside the door heralded Issy's debut and made talking impossible.

The street band was brilliant. Out of what Issy feared was a totally incompatible bunch of individuals, she and the percussion leader, a manic stringy figure with a mane of frizzy black hair, had created an exuberant hip-swaying unit, whose wild brass and heart-stirring rhythms had even me on my feet.

"Fucking ace," I said to Issy as I rushed to embrace her after their set, "that was fucking ace."

"I must admit," she said, glowing as if she was about to internally combust, "that was the most fun I've had vertical for years. I'd forgotten what a buzz it is to play for an audience." Her gaze left mine to travel the hall, and by the flash of joy in her smile, I knew that she and Eleanor had made eye contact.

That was probably the high point of the evening. I saw Issy and Amy exchange frozen greetings, then Issy went to hang out with her band, while I sat uncomfortably with the others through a truly appalling comic, a report on BAG's progress so far and a couple of other enthusiastic clunky acts, until Bill's arrival meant I had an excuse to leave, pleading technical details which needed sorting. Of course, this meant telling him all the scandal, and we amused ourselves quite adequately in the interval. I was running around the grotty corridors backstage, looking for a lead I had carelessly put down somewhere, when I nearly charged into Issy and Eleanor, who were standing a few feet apart from each other, both looking as if they were on the verge of tears. In spite of slamming on my anchors and retreating, I couldn't avoid overhearing their unhappy mutterings.

"I must go," Issy was saying, "I must go."

"I don't want you to." Eleanor's voice was intense, "At least come with me somewhere for a coffee. We must talk."

"No." Issy was being desperately firm, "There's nothing to talk about while you're with Amy."

She fled through a fire exit, and I saw Eleanor screw up her face and stumble off in the direction of the main hall. Hell, I thought as the pain in their exchange hit me, hell, hell, hell, this isn't fun any more. Oddly unsettled, I managed to find the lead and to give a creditable performance to the by now mainly drunk crowd. I was glad to finish, even if I was going home to an empty house. While I was packing away my things and taking hefty swigs from a pint of vodka and tonic, thoughtfully provided by Fred, I noticed Jeanie, bottle of beer in hand, lurching unsteadily towards me. There was no sign of Alison.

"Kate," she hiccupped and tried to smile, "have you seen Issy?"

"She left ages ago," I said absently, coiling up the offending lead, "before we started, I think."

"Oh no," her normally jovial face crumpled, and I realised that not only was she under the influence, she was very upset as well, "oh no, I wanted a lift back home to Kirktown with her. I can't go on the bike like this."

I was tired and had had enough of the evening, but I couldn't quell a rush of concern. "Hang on," I said, and put the lead with the rest of the electrical junk, "what's wrong? Where's Alison?"

"Oh Kate," her voice quavered. Surely she wasn't going to burst into tears on me? "Oh Kate." Yes she was. "It's all gone wrong, we're over and I've nowhere to go." She sat down quickly on the sticky floor, not letting go of her beer, and bowed her head. I kicked a cigarette butt out of the way, and knelt beside her,

"Oh don't cry chuck," I put my arm over her shoulders, "don't cry. You can come back with me and tell me all about it."

She lifted her flushed tear-streaked face, topped by its tufts of fair hair, looking for all the world like a distressed child. "Oh Kate," she repeated, "can I? Thanks. . ." Her words faded away into more tears, and she sat there, alternately crying and slurping beer, through my hurried packing and farewells.

Her woeful tale came out in between sniffs and wails as we staggered back to the house. She had assumed, without spelling it out, that Alison would stay around in the long summer vacation, "I wanted her to live in my flat with me in Kirktown, she could get a job easy, it would be spot on." Alison, however, had other plans, and had announced that she would be going back to her parents in Norfolk instead. "So I chucked her," Jeanie moaned, "she doesn't love me, does she? Not if she wants to spend all the summer away from me."

I was about the worst qualified person to give an opinion on that one. "It doesn't mean she doesn't love you at all," I said anyway, "maybe her parents are putting pressure on her to come home. . ."

"That's another thing," Jeanie had worked her way into belligerence, "she won't tell them about me. But my mum and dad have had her for tea and everything."

"Oh Jeanie," I tightened my arm around her, "not everyone's parents are as easy as yours and mine."

By the time we had got home, she had lapsed into heartbreak again, and I put her on the sofa.

"Where's Liz?" she asked in a pause in her wailing, "what've you got to drink here?"

"Away for the night, and you've had enough," I said strictly and hypocritically, "I'm going to make you some coffee."

"Spoilsport," I heard her mutter. A mite unsteady on my own pins from my hastily downed vodka, I rather untidily made some coffee and sat down next to her, doing my inadequate best to convince her that it wasn't necessarily over with Alison. Even if it was, she would recover and fall in love again, because no-one I knew had succumbed to a broken heart at the tender age of twenty and never lived to make the same mistake all over again.

"Oh Kate," she murmured eventually, leaning into me, "you're so kind. So warm and cuddly."

It felt comfortable, and I was wondering if I might have preferred to be described as sensual and alluring, when she sat more upright, and looked straight at me,

"And you're beautiful, you know, with that fantastic hair." Her diction had improved immeasurably.

I stared back. There was no mistaking the invitation in her squiffy blue eyes, or in her practised hand brushing my curls. The forgotten wings of temptation fluttered inside me. She was young and attractive, and I knew for an instant how nice she'd be. Perhaps it would do no harm, some happy uncomplicated sex with none of the heavy emotional baggage that seemed to be clinging round Liz and me these days. . . I recoiled in horror.

"Jesus, Jeanie!" I bit back my appalled exclamations. "Don't be daft," I said gently, "I'm far too old for this, I'm with Liz and anyway, you're pissed."

"OK, it was worth a try," she said equably and settled back again, "are you going to make me sleep down here?"

"You can have the spare room," I said, starting to giggle,

"and no sneaking into my bed in the small hours."

"Don't worry," her eyelids were already drooping, "I can take no for an answer. I know you're a woman of integurr. . . inte-something."

It took all of my declining strength to get her upstairs and to install her in the spare room, which was really a repository for everything we couldn't find a place for, before I flopped down in the bleakness of my lonely bed, hoping that the prevailing storms in everyone else's love life weren't contagious.

I woke far earlier than I would have liked the next day, with no Liz beside me to lull me back to sleep or to persuade on to more active pleasures. I didn't hear a squeak from the spare room as I showered, got dressed, had some tea and toast and a cigarette, then had an ineffectual go at clearing up downstairs. The knock at the door startled me from a discussion with myself on whether I still needed every piece of violin music from Grade 1 upwards, and I had to paste a welcoming smile on my alarmed features when I saw Amy standing there.

"Hi, how nice to see you," I said insincerely, "come in, I'll put the kettle on."

"Just passing," she said with equal falseness, "thought it was about time I saw where you were living now."

"You may not believe it, but I'm actually tidying up at the moment," I said brightly, leading her to the dining area, "I'm amazed at how much stuff we accumulate. Tea? Coffee?"

"Coffee would be lovely," she said, moving a pair of shoes from one of the chairs, "Liz not around?"

"Oh, she was away last night at a family do," I said carelessly, "she'll be back early this afternoon."

She waited until I had made the coffee, sat down and rolled another cigarette before she pounced.

"All right, Kate," she said, all the artifice gone from her voice, "what's going on?"

I dropped my lighter. "What do you mean?" I said from under the table.

"You know what I mean," she scowled at me as I emerged from the floor, "Eleanor and Issy. How long has it been going on?"

"Nothing's going on," I blustered, "they're both involved with BAG of course. . ." I blew out a smokescreen.

"Don't lie to me, Kate." I jumped at her harshness. "Issy still hasn't forgiven me, and all she wants to do is cause trouble between me and Eleanor."

I remembered Issy's distress the previous night, and was furiously angry.

"How dare you, Amy! I know Issy, and she would never behave like that. . ." My developing tirade was stopped by a plaintive cry from the bottom of the stairs.

"Ka-ate, can I have a shower and some tea?" It was Jeanie, wrapped naked in a sheet, her hair ruffled and her eyes bloodshot. She took a few wobbly steps towards us, like a young Roman emperor the morning after a successful orgy.

"Oh chicken." I stood up to put the kettle on again, "Of course. God, you look rough, have some water." I filled a pint glass, and walked over to put it in her shaky hand.

"Ta," she said, and drank most of it. "Psst," she hissed and motioned with her head to the hall, "I need a word."

"What?" I said, trying not to laugh, once we had moved out of Amy's beady range of vision. Jeanie had gone bright red.

"Did I, er, come on to you last night? I can't quite remember. . ." she whispered.

"Um, sort of," I found myself sniggering, "but don't worry, nothing happened."

She looked mortified, "I'm sorry, that was awful of me. When you took me in. . ."

"Oh sweetie, don't torture yourself," I grinned, "I was flattered."

"Really?" She began to smile, then her face dropped in anguish, "Are you going to tell Liz? She'll kill me."

"Of course I won't tell Liz," I promised. "Now go and have a shower, and I'll make your tea." I planted a kiss on her troubled brow, and turned to see Amy standing behind me.

"I'm off," she said bluntly, "I can see it's no good expecting you to help."

It didn't occur to me to try to work out what she meant.

I had another breakfast with Jeanie before she left to find her bike, pottered around some more, sorted out something to wear for the reception that evening and even ironed it before a walk in the park. I had a little worry about the tangle Issy, Eleanor and Amy seemed to be in, pictured Liz speeding impatiently back up the motorway to me, and allowed myself a small anticipatory frisson. With hindsight, it was a good thing I ran into Bill on my meandering way out of the main gates.

"Kate!" he said, looking chuffed, "there's a lucky thing. I was coming to your place for a copy of that bloody horrible new tune we're trying tonight. I've lost mine, and I want to check a few things out for me twiddles."

"Fine." I tried to be tactful, "Um, Liz may be back. . ."

"Well, I'll just hang around for ages then, so you don't use up all your energy for tonight in unnatural acts. What're you wearing? Are you going smart?"

"Of course, I'm going to look prettier than you," I said, and we bitched away at each other until we reached the end of our street. I scanned the lines of parked cars with no rusty Fiesta among them, and felt the disappointed jolt in my chest. Maybe she'd left Bath later than she intended. As soon as I walked into the house, however, I knew she'd been back and had gone out again. My mind struggled with what I saw. A packet of photos she'd taken to show to her family lay on the floor, one of my paperbacks she'd borrowed was in the fireplace, and a pair of her earrings, specially chosen by me, rested on a pile of letters by the phone, as if she'd pulled them out while making a call. Why did I feel as if I'd been shot? I shook my head, to get rid of the buzzing, and found myself in the kitchen. Propped against Liz's favourite mug was a piece of paper bearing three words in her large handwriting. I picked the mug and paper up, blinking and squinting at the incomprehensible message.

"What does this say?" I asked Bill, handing him the note.

The bones of his face stood out like a carving of Death in a medieval cathedral. "Gone to Sylv's," he whispered, and I let the mug fall to the tiled floor.

Mercifully, the next hours are a bit of a blur in my memory. I know that Bill made a brief phone call, forced me to put my outfit for the evening in a bag and pick up my violin, and then walked me round to Pat's. Numb from the neck down, which in any other circumstances would have been interesting, I prattled away to him, convinced my brain had finally caught up with what was going on.

"Well, I knew it would happen sooner or later," I said firmly, "she's got fed up with me like she's got fed up with every woman she's been with, and gone back to her stand-by lover Sylv in London. Just as well, really, though I'll have to find someone else to share the house with me. Shouldn't be too hard. I'll start packing up her stuff tonight after the gig, and if she gives me half the money for the car, that'll be fair. . ."

Bill said nothing, only held my hand as tightly as if I was a zeppelin he had to keep tethered to the earth.

Pat opened the door, and I went automatically to her familiar kitchen.

"Back where I started, hey?" I said cheerily to her white face, "Shall I put the kettle on?"

I glanced at her corkboard, and saw a photo of Liz and me I didn't know she had. Someone must have taken it without us noticing while we were fooling around in the back garden during the brief autumn weeks we had lived in the flat upstairs. In it we were looking intently at each other, clearly about to kiss.

"Shit," I said as my heart cracked as irrevocably as the mug, "I think I'm going to be sick."

I spent the afternoon throwing up and trying to prevent myself from sliding into the ocean of grief and despair which lapped at my ankles, waiting for the moment when my guard slipped and it could claim me for ever.

"I don't believe it," Pat kept saying, "Liz loves you. I know she does."

"No she doesn't, not any more," I repeated dry-eyed, "and I'm playing tonight. She can't take that from me as well."

How I did it, I still don't know, yet I changed, got into the shocked and silent van when it came round to pick me up, and contributed to the muted discussion on how we were going to manage the mechanics of the evening. The numbness had returned, and I gave no more than a passing attention to remembering the conversation Pat and I had had before I left.

"It's happening to everyone," I had said in the hall, "I had to give Jeanie a bed last night because she finished with Alison, and Amy turned up this morning to bug me about Issy and Eleanor."

Pat's eyes had narrowed. "Hang on in there, Kate," she had said, giving me a tentative hug, "I'm going to find out what's going on."

I hope the boisterous wedding crowd didn't catch on that the fiddle player in the band, instead of being a functioning human, was a badly programmed automaton which chose the moment the music came to an end to flip out of suspended animation and start crying. I sobbed and sobbed behind the marquee while the others did all the work of packing up, and, too sunk in overwhelming loss to be embarrassed, couldn't stop through the long drive back to Pat's.

"I'm staying here with you," Bill announced, "Pat said she'd make up the spare room for us," and I wasn't even able to thank him for practically carrying me into the house and up the stairs.

It was probably the worst night I have ever spent, and I've had a few horrors. Worse certainly than the first night I spent alone after I'd left Chloe's house, and worse than the nights after I'd left Liz in France, not knowing if I'd see her again. I hated Liz more than I would have believed possible, and I longed for her with every cell in my body. How could she leave me like this? Why hadn't I gone with her to the party, like she wanted, then none of this would have happened. I'd blown it. It's all been a waste, I told myself, listening to Bill breathing on a mattress on the floor next to me, the fighting, the laughs, the hours and hours of loving each other in bed. A nightmare vision of Liz's mouth on Sylv span unbidden into my mind, and I had to rush to the bathroom again. So this was how Issy had felt when she found out about Bel and Amy. I'd have to put up with years of misery like hers until I recovered, by which time I would be too old to attract anyone.

I don't know if Bill got any rest, and I was convinced I would never sleep again, but I must have done, because it was suddenly broad daylight, and there was Pat, mug of tea in hand, sitting on my bed. She was smiling.

"Admire me," she said, trying not to look too pleased with herself, "I've solved the mystery of the disappearing lover and, yes, you can smoke in here by special dispensation." She ignored the ashtray I'd nearly filled with damp fag ends in the night.

"What?" I said muzzily.

"I've just been speaking to Eleanor on the phone." Pat put my fingers round the mug's handle, "Listen carefully, lovey, you'll find this hard to believe. El was out for most of yesterday, and when she came back, Amy told her that she'd found out that you and Jeanie had spent the night together, and so she'd phoned Liz in the afternoon to tell her. She must have caught Liz just when she got back from Bath while you were out."

"What?"

Pat raised her voice, "Amy saw Jeanie at your house yesterday morning, and she told Liz that you and Jeanie had slept together. That's why Liz must have got the hump and bombed off to London."

I felt my eyes revolve in my head. "But why?" I croaked, "Why would Amy do that? It's ludicrous."

"She's jealous," Bill's voice came from somewhere under his quilt, "she's jealous of what you and Liz have. If you ask me," his head appeared, "she's flipped. As they say in psychiatric circles. She looked nuts to me on Friday."

I started crying again. It hadn't been a bad dream after all. "It makes no difference," I wept, "if Liz believes I'd do that, and has been with Sylv again, I can't go back to her."

Pat looked at me, her sympathy turned down a notch or two.

"Did you, Kate?" she asked.

"Did I what?"

"Sleep with Jeanie."

"No!" I yelled snottily, "How could you think I'd. . ." I met her eyes, "No," I said, much more quietly, "I was tempted, but I didn't."

"Good." She gave my legs a brisk rub, "Now, here's Sylv's number. Don't ask how it came into my possession. If I were you, I'd have a nice bath then ring up and see what's going on with Liz."

"I can't," I cried even more, "I can't face her."

"OK." Pat got up off the bed, "Either do something to sort this, or spend the rest of your life crying here. It's your choice. Mind you," she gave me her kindest smile, "I'll charge you rent again. Got to make some Sunday pancakes for Tom and Ag, if she's surfaced." She skipped out of the

107

room, as if the total ruin of my life was no more than a collapsed souffle.

"She's right," Bill said, "and if I know her, she spent all of yesterday night phoning round your friends till she got at the truth. I'm not trying to guilt trip you, but perhaps you could do a little. . ."

"Fuck off," I said, threw a pillow at his head, and shivered into the bathroom.

"And I see being with Liz hasn't improved your manners," he shouted after me.

Half an hour later, I was retching by the phone, having realised that I wasn't going to die, and would have to speak to Liz. Sylv answered, and even recognised that I was speaking English.

"Is Liz there?" I crackled, unable to get any moisture in my mouth.

"Nah. It's Kate, isn't it?" she drawled, "she's on her way back."

"Oh." In a million years, I could never ask what I needed to know.

"Yeah," she continued lazily, "when you see her, tell her not to come running to me with her fucking problems. I've got my own life to deal with."

"Oh."

"Bloody hell, woman," her tone was momentarily more friendly than her words, "we didn't do anything, though even if we did, can't see why you're so worked up. You've got her where you want her."

The floor slipped with relief under my feet, I dropped the receiver back on its cradle and contrived to burst into yet more tears.

12

I refused Pat's offer of pancakes, which was probably the only time I'd ever turned down her cooking, avoided Tom and Ag, and walked queasily home, hoping I'd thanked Bill enough for sticking with me. My head was thick, my heart pounded and I knew nothing was solved. Sylv might have been lying, Liz trusted me so little that she'd believed Amy's tittle tattle without bothering to check if it was true, and I might never be able to forgive her for rushing off like that. Was it worth it, when I let her cause me so much misery? I paced the house, mainlining tea and nicotine, until the sound of Liz's key in the lock sent a wave of something like fear galloping through me. I made myself sit on the sofa and wait. She stood in the doorway, her face looking peculiarly dreadful, as if it had been smashed into careless shards then put back together again by a short-sighted potter.

"I came back," she said hoarsely, her eyes avoiding mine.

"So I see," I replied, horrified at the hard even tone of my voice.

She sagged against the door-jamb. "Well," she tried to shrug, "was it a one-off, or is it an on-going thing?"

For a moment, I had no idea what she meant. "I'm sorry?" I said, a shadow of a squeak breaking into my question.

She shut her eyes and clenched her fists. "You and Jeanie." She wasn't even shouting, "Is it. . ."

Rage hit me like a number 7 bus. Now I knew why domestic murders were committed. "Fucksake," if I kept sitting down, I wouldn't run the risk of strangling her, "how could you believe Amy? Why did you rush off like that? Why didn't you wait, I was only in the park. . ." I carried on, and they heard two streets away that I hadn't slept with Jeanie but wished I had because it might have made up for the torture I'd suffered.

"Oh," she slumped in a chair, her face in her hands, "I couldn't do it with Sylv. I tried, but it was crap."

I couldn't understand why she wasn't getting angry as well.

"Good." I kicked my ashtray over, "Why, Liz, why did you

listen to Amy? What kind of person do you think I am? How can this work if you don't trust me. . ." I stopped when she lifted her head and I saw the tears in her eyes. My heart turned over, very slowly. She'd only ever once cried properly in front of me, and that was during the first night we were together.

"Kate," I had to strain to hear her, "it all just made sense, what Amy said. I know I'm not that. . .easy to be with, and I thought. . .I always thought you might prefer someone nicer. I just didn't think I'd feel so bad, I had to get away, and could only think of Sylv's. She sent me back. . ."

"Liz!" I did a clumsy version of yogic flying across the room and landed squashily at her feet, making a desperate grab for her limp hands, "Liz, darling heart, don't you know I really love you? I love being with you, you're the best thing that ever happened to me. . ." Crying as well, I poured out in an unstoppable flood all the pent-up endearments I'd never quite dared to utter before, and somehow grappled her to the floor, where I held her, stroking her back, until I felt the tension ebbing away from her stiff shoulders and spine, and the warmth returning to her skin.

"Oh babe," she snuffled eventually, "I didn't want to believe Amy, I wasn't sure how you felt, I was so confused. . ." She yawned abruptly, "I'm tired."

I realised that she had spent most of the last three days going up and down the motorway, with a major wobbler in the middle.

"Sweetest," I held her closer, "I'll run you a bath, then you can have a rest and we can sort everything out later." All my warring feelings were being swamped by a longing for nothing more than sleep.

She sighed. Her body had never felt so helplessly lax. "I threw up over someone's car in the motorway services," she said in a small voice.

"I threw up all yesterday afternoon," I replied. "Not that it's a competition," I added kindly. The awfulness of the previous night was fast receding.

"What a fucking mess." She buried her face in my shoulder again, "Do you think we need therapy?"

"No, we need a snooze. And then we can see how we um . . . feel." Even then, I wasn't sure if desire could return from beyond this exhausted calm. I had just been telling her how much I adored her, yet now I knew she had tried to sleep with Sylv, would it ever work for me again?

"Don't you have to go out?" The weariness in her tone nearly had me weeping once more. Ages ago I had promised to play with another band in a pub session that night.

"I'll ring up and say I'm ill," I said, my words slurring with fatigue, "I can't play like this."

I got through to Mac, the main man of the pub band while Liz was in the bath, and he was very annoyed.

"You promised," he said, "we arranged this weeks ago. Couldn't you have told me sooner?"

"I'm sorry," I said over and over again, "I'm not well. I thought I'd feel better if I left it, but I don't." I wasn't going to go into any detail about my personal life. He slammed the phone down in disgust. I weakened. Now I would get a reputation for being unreliable, this could be really harmful, I could make sure Liz was ok and come back early, I might be able to stay awake, should I ring back. . . The phone trilled telepathically.

"Er, Kate?" It was Dave, sounding awkward.

"Oh, hi."

"Look, I know this probably isn't a good time. . ."

"'S'ok, Liz's back, we're sort of working it out, you know." What the hell did he want? I could hear Liz walking into the bedroom.

"Yeah. I only wanted to say. . .you did really well last night, considering. I thought you were very professional." He paused, "And the others haven't put me up to this. Bye."

This, from the person in the band who was always the most critical of me. It was like getting an Oscar. So nuts to you, Mac, I thought, and crawled upstairs to see if I could slip into bed next to Liz. She was lying, stiff again, on her back with her eyes closed. In a final wave of sickness, the thought that she had probably shared a bed with Sylv last night gagged in my throat. I got in anyway, and for a while we remained motionless, like a crusader and his wife on their tomb, before she turned her head a fraction towards me. Her breathing reached mine, her eyes flickered briefly open and, with a moan, she rolled over. As if it was a normal night, not the afternoon of our deepest crisis, we eased into the way we usually went to sleep, arms over each other and legs folded together.

"I'm sorry," she whispered, "let's not do that again in a hurry."

Shreds of anguish seeped out of my heart and I drifted towards sleep.

It was night outside when I woke up. Liz had switched on the bedside lamp and was looking at me, her old smile curving along her mouth and her eyes dark and soft. She slid her hand up me to stroke my cheek, and a blissful current purled through to my pelvis.

"Hey," she said.

"Hey," I replied.

Her hair was alive under my fingers, and the light touch of her mouth on mine was the sweetest thing I have ever tasted. Soon nothing mattered apart from what we could do together. We stared at each other, so close I felt that it was my lungs breathing the air in and out of her heaving chest, and her heart sending the fizzing blood pulsing round inside me.

"I meant what I said," Liz mumbled the next morning when we were having breakfast in bed. After about ten seconds of mature reflection, we had decided that cancelling our pressing engagements and spending the day working out what had gone wrong between us, then beginning the hard slog of rebuilding our relationship, would be the grown up thing to do. Equally seriously, we had resolved that this would involve putting the blame on Amy, and not getting up for the foreseeable future.

"Which bit?" I asked, upending the sugar bowl over my rice krispies, "The bit about my buttocks being like the full moon, my skin like cream, my. . ."

"OK, ok," she slopped milk around, "I was just trying to be poetic. You said some lovely things to me as well. No, the bit about, you know, being in love with you."

"Good," I attempted to give her shoulder a little lick without upsetting my bowl, "I'm in love with you." I enjoyed watching her blush.

"Yeah, well, I mean," she stuffed some cornflakes in her mouth and continued inarticulately, "you know I've always wanted you like mad in bed, more than anyone for years, and it's nice living with you and all that stuff, you're good fun. But," she swallowed desperately, "I suppose I assumed that eventually we'd go off each other and move on, like you do."

"Hm."

"God, I wish this was easier." She chewed away some more, "It's only that lately I've been feeling. . .I've been feeling, especially since that bastard at the BAG camp made you cry, that I'd like to try. . . like to try to stay with you for a long time, and make it work and even have a go at being faithful and all that kind of. . ." She risked a glance at me. "Are you laughing at me?" she demanded crossly.

"No," I sniffed, "I think I'm going to cry again."

"You'll spoil your rice krispies," she said and put an arm round me, balancing her cornflakes on her thighs. "One thing, though," she whiffled into my hair, "in return for my unique promise of an attempt at fidelity, you have to tell me what you really want to do with that massage oil."

I whispered into her ear, and was rewarded by a groan and an involuntary spasm which tipped soggy cornflakes everywhere.

"Jesus," she said, "can you eat a bit faster?"

I could have been forgiven for thinking that life would now settle down. After a day of wild excess and disgusting soppiness, we lay back, temporarily sated, surveying the wreck we'd made of the bedroom.

"D'you think our relationship's back on track?" I asked, trying to stop laughing.

"I hope so," Liz picked a cornflake out of my hair, "the fixtures and fittings won't take much more of this. I know," she put her hand back on my breast, "why don't we have a little tidy up and go out for a drink? We've been in here for over twenty four hours."

"Are you bored of me already?" I pretended to whine. "Aren't I enough for you? Besides," I remembered, "I can't go anywhere where I'll see anybody. I'm ill."

"We could go to the Grand," she said. "We could pretend you're married and we're having a secret passionate affair. Wear a skirt and look nervous."

"Blimey," I looked at her in amazement, "is this one of your fantasies?" The Grand was the last smart hotel in the city

113

centre, and was the favourite of expense account businessmen and what remained of the county set.

"One of the more decent ones," she snickered, "I'll have to introduce you to them gradually."

Diverted, I pulled her closer, "Tell me another."

"Later," she said, her mouth smiling on mine, "but one of them involves substantial quantities of strawberries and whipped cream."

"Oh wow, food as well," I gave her a contemplative kiss, "I'll go shopping tomorrow."

Once we'd got out of the house, I realised that it was a beautiful evening. Wisps of apricot cloud scrolled across the sky, the trees were bursting with bright new leaves, and layers of blossom scent hung in the warm placid air. Walking beside Liz, I tried to pin down the unusual sensation swelling in my chest along with love, happiness, physical satisfaction and general joy at the world. It took me several minutes to recognise that I felt secure. I gave a little jump, and took Liz's hand.

"Don't beat Jeanie up, will you?" I said. I'd broken my promise to the poor girl, and told Liz every detail of what had happened.

"Nah. She's no worse than me. I might drop dark hints and let her stew, though," she said, then coughed. "Um, Kate?"

"Yes?"

"I know you've no reason to like Sylv, and it's not as if you're likely to meet her again, but. . .don't think too badly of her. She was all right when I turned up. . ."

"OK," I could afford to be magnanimous "so long as you promise to burn all your photos of her, never let a thought of her cross your mind, and never ever mention her name again in my presence. . ."

We traded punches for old times' sake, and went into the Grand.

"Right," Liz said in a low voice, as if we were planning a bank robbery, "let's get into role. You go and sit down and look paranoid, and I'll go to the bar."

Eager to please, I minced into the faded opulence of the lounge bar and sat, ankles crossed, in one of the huge armchairs. The old fashioned chandelier style light fittings could have done with a polish, and the carpet was a bit worn in places, but it was still several cuts above the pubs we usually frequented. It was also virtually empty, apart from a solitary man a few tables away from me and a couple of blue-rinsed elderly ladies sipping sherry in a corner. I started scratting for my tobacco then realised that rolling cigarettes might not be in character, so I smoothed my skirt and fluttered my eyelashes at Liz as she came back from the bar.

"Here you are, darling," she said gruffly, and put a drink with a parasol in on a little doily in front of me. "It's some kind of vodka cocktail," she explained out of the corner of her mouth, sitting down with a bottle of lager opposite me.

"Thank you," I quavered, and took a genteel sip. I shoved my papers, tobacco and lighter under the table on to her lap, "Roll me one of your cigarettes, would you? I'm so tense."

"Oh darling," her capable fingers handed me the neatly rolled tube, "why can't you leave him?" She clicked the lighter for me, and I cupped her hand in mine.

"I would this minute if it wasn't for the children." I sighed dramatically, "And my family just wouldn't understand. . ." I sat back and inhaled sadly.

"We could go away from here." She leaned forward and clutched my hand, "We can make a new start somewhere where no-one knows us."

"Fate is so cruel, my precious," I was getting into this, "why is our love forbidden?"

"I can be strong for both of us," she growled, "hold on to our dream."

It was too much. Bubbles from my drink went up my nose, and my neighs of laughter made the barman look up from his newspaper.

"You horror," Liz wiped her eyes, "I hope you don't do this to all my fantasies."

We beamed with pleasure at each other.

"I forgot to ask," she said, relaxing back into her chair, "how was the benefit night?"

"Issy's band were fantastic, the rest was fairly crap." I downed my odd tasting drink, "How was the party?"

"Nice." She looked at me from under her eyebrows, "I wish you'd been able to be there."

"So do I," I said automatically, and that set us off again.

"How could I have been so stupid, believing Amy like

that?" she said after a while, "I thought you were the jealous one."

"I am," I said, "I couldn't bear the thought of you and Sylv . . ."

"Don't," her foot reached mine, "I'm just as bad as you, really. I um," she looked embarrassed, "I don't exactly get bored when you're away, you know. I can usually find stuff to do, and I know I can always go for a drink with the girls and I'm used to my own company. It's only hard when I find myself thinking that maybe you've found someone else. . .oh fuck," she started tearing at a beer mat, "that's why I came down early when you were in Wales." She gave a little grin, "Besides wanting you like hell, of course."

It was suddenly easy to be honest, "Is it because I used to sleep around a bit when Chloe and I were splitting up?" She nodded, and I let my hand travel to her knee. "That was then," I said, "I wouldn't do that now."

We had another session of beaming, then I plunged in, "I was afraid you meant us as well when you said that Eleanor and Amy should split up."

"God, no," she looked astonished, "we're not like that. I wonder if Eleanor will see sense after Amy's meddling. . . That man over there, who's been staring at us, he's a stringer."

"A what?" I squinched round to see him.

"A stringer. He ferrets around and gets in touch with the national papers with any news he thinks might interest them."

"How do you know?" I recalled how long it had taken me to feel settled in the north, and realised how quickly she'd been able to find her own life here.

"Through Ben." He was the photographer she did jobs for. "They go drinking together, and talk about the story that'll give them their big break."

"Maybe this is where the local mafia meet, and he's on to some scandal about refuse collection contracts." We all liked to assume, in spite of the complete lack of evidence, that the city council was a hotbed of intrigue and corruption.

"Someone's just come to join him. He doesn't look like a godfather, though."

I put my head discreetly round the wings of my armchair

116

to see a short, vaguely familiar figure shake hands with the stringer and motion with his arm back to the lobby. The two men disappeared, and, after a few seconds, in the hush of the nearly empty bar I heard the ping of a lift door opening.

"That was Jack!" Liz clicked her fingers in recognition, "You remember, Issy's neighbour, the one who minds Tam. We should have said hello."

"He might not have wanted to know us in public," I said, "especially since that stringer's seen us having hysterics. Shall we have another drink, or do you want to wander home? I've got to recover from my malady by tomorrow, I'm meant to be in the studio again."

"Wander home, I think." She held out a hand to pull me up, "At least I can tick that fantasy off my list."

13

Bog-eyed and walking about two feet off the ground, I made it to the studio on time. We were meant to be recording some authentic-sounding diddly-dee music for a lurid tourist video, and when I sneaked in, the others were apparently discussing the most potent and disastrous drinks they'd tried.

"A punch made from white wine, vermouth and dry cider," Jo was saying, "I was paralysed for about eight hours."

"That Tunisian spirit made from figs. I underwent a personality change and started punching a wall." Bill looked up at my discreet entrance, "Hello, Kate, hear you and Liz have made up. Enjoying the honeymoon?"

I decided to brazen it out. "Yes, thank you," I said courteously, "though I can't remember phoning you to tell you all the details."

"Don't look at me," Dave said defensively, "I'm the soul of discretion."

Bill laughed, "Actually, Pat said she happened to be walking by your house yesterday afternoon. She knocked but there was no reply, so she drew her own conclusions from the closed curtains. And I hear you never made it to play with that other band."

"You can't do anything in this town," I started attacking the vending machine to hide my blushes, "I'm afraid Mac's not best pleased with me. Still, my life should be nice and calm from now on."

"I wouldn't be too sure of that," Fred gave an embarrassed smile, "I was just telling the others. This American thing's on if we want in. Six months starting next March, going round with a bunch of other bands. It'll mean we miss the summer festivals here, of course." He scratched his head and looked worried, as if he was afraid I was going to hit him.

"OK," I sat down with my flimsy cup, "how long can you all give me before I make a final decision? And I promise I'll stick to it and not moan or anything. Well," I thought I'd better be realistic, "no more than normal, anyway."

They breathed a collective sigh of relief, and I knew they'd been mulling this over before I arrived.

"End of June?" Fred said hesitantly. "You know we want you to come with us, but we'll understand if you decide to stay here. That should give us enough time to put out feelers and find someone else, not that anyone can replace you. . ."

"Let's face it, Kate," Dave said, getting out his guitar and twanging a loud chord, "you're a weirdo and a pain in the butt, and I'd much prefer some beautiful young thing in a low-cut dress, so say no and give me a break." The certainty that he didn't mean a word of it warmed the cockles of my already over-heated heart.

"All right," I said, "that does it. I'm going to ask around the scene. There's a lovely retired music teacher I know who plays a mean violin." We talked rubbish until it was time to start.

All this levity didn't make my dilemma easier to contemplate. Now that the tour was definite, I'd have to bring it up with Liz, and I sensed that I would have to do it right away. I would tell her about it that very evening, even if it put a spanner into the works of our deciding we were in love, made for each other and would never fight again. When I got back to the house, she was lying on the floor, her feet up on a chair, talking, or rather listening, to someone on the phone.

"El," she mouthed at me as I came in, and she reached up with her hand to pull me down beside her. I lay close, so I could feel the vibrations of her scattered "yes's", "noes", and "of courses", and mirror the smile forming at the corners of her mouth when I walked my fingers up her thighs and round her waistband.

"No, it's Kate," she said, after a particularly sharp intake of breath, "she's fooling around here." She covered the mouthpiece, "El says hi and sorry about Amy," she relayed.

"Say hi and don't worry back," I said, and resolved to spend at least fifteen minutes every day kissing her ears.

Liz passed on the message, listened some more, and moved one leg off the chair. I progressed to her neck. "Well, one of us will of course, but why don't you. . .?" she said, gasped, and rolled her eyes at Eleanor's reply. "OK," she said finally, "Take care, see you soon, love to Toni."

"Mm. . .mm. . .," she tried to kiss and talk at the same time, "Eleanor's moved out and is staying with Toni for a while. . . this is nice, I'm glad it's half term and I've no classes tonight. . . though she says Issy won't have anything to do with her until she and Amy have definitely split and she wants one of us to ring her and check she's all right, we should go upstairs. . .ah, God," the complex rhythms of desire were weaving us tighter, "Let's just. . ."

We snaked along the floor to the dining area out of sight of the window, and enjoyed ourselves among the chair legs and sundry other items of furniture.

"That was fun," I said, brushing crumbs off my legs, "apart from the carpet burns."

Liz laughed even more, and stroked the sole of my foot with her toes, "I'd have hoovered if I'd known. I think it would be nice on the stairs as well, With gravity and all."

I bent my head to her stomach for a while, breathing in her musky perfume. It was now or never. "Liz," I muttered, "please, please don't go all withdrawn on me. I have to tell you this," I bumbled it out, ending with, "and they've given me till the end of June to decide whether I'm going with them."

She stiffened, and her eyes retreated. "Go if you want," she said evenly, reaching for her shirt, "I don't want to hold you back."

I kept my eyes on hers, "The way I feel now, I don't want to go away for so long." She didn't waver. "But I want to talk about it properly," I stumbled on, "I want to be sure I'm doing the right thing for me."

"Sweetheart," she had come back and was meeting me half-way, "we'll talk about it as much as you want, we've got loads of time really. What's more important at this moment is whether you're going to phone Issy while I do some cooking, or," she put a fingertip to my mouth, "you're going to take me upstairs and soften the blow of what you've just told me by indulging me some more."

"You just want a sex slave." I gave her fingertip what I thought was my most sensual kiss, "OK, as long as you cook my tea afterwards."

I phoned Issy while Liz was being efficient in the kitchen. If I craned my neck, I could catch glimpses of her chopping and frying, and swishing around in the loose middle-eastern robe she sometimes wore.

"Kate," Issy sounded worn, "I heard you and Liz had a terrible bust-up because of something Amy did. What's going on?"

I reassured her, and gave her the bare bones of what had happened. There was a silence.

"Issy?" I pushed, "Why won't you talk to Eleanor? She wants to know how you are."

"Oh hell," she was sounding worse by the minute, "I just don't want to get involved until she's sure. . .I know she's at Toni's, but that's not only because she was pissed off with Amy. It's this bloody Bradley Boltons thing, she was getting a creepy feeling at their house, like it was being watched, and stuff was happening. Calls in the middle of the night, and neighbours saying they'd seen people hanging round."

"God," I was shocked, "what's she got into?" I had a sudden vision of the young security guard, and felt nauseous.

"I don't know. She rang yesterday and mumbled something I didn't understand about loans and investment, but that was when I told her I wasn't going to carry on like this, so it wasn't exactly a long conversation after that."

"Have you. . .?" How could I put this delicately?

She caught my drift. "No. Not that I don't want to, mind."

She became a little more her cynical self, "I'm practising restraint, and anyway, it's odd to feel this way about her after all these years, could be a bonkers phase I'm going through . . .ooh," she'd obviously remembered something, "Jeanie and Alison have made up, Jeanie's decided to go all mature and put up with Alison going to Norfolk. Hang on," I heard a distant bang, "that's Jack at the door, I think, probably with yet another moan against Bolton's. I'll have to go."

"Ask him what he was doing with that reporter in the Grand in town last night," I said, "we saw him when we were having a drinks break."

"The old devil," Issy had cheered up, "I knew he was lying when I saw him getting out his lethal car, and he said he was going to a whist drive in Kirktown. I must go and interrogate him. See you soon, I hope."

"Yes, see you," I rang off, and went to harass Liz.

"All right." Liz put something wonderful looking in front of me, "Talk to me. What do you think'll happen to us if you go to the States?"

"I don't know. I'll be utterly miserable, you'll realise you're happier without me and find someone else. That's my worst case scenario," I explained, "you've been rolling your eyes all evening."

"If I find someone else, which I've no immediate intention of doing thank you very much, it could happen just as easily when you're here. And," she jabbed at me with her fork, "in spite of what you seem to believe, I can go without sex for six months."

"Can you?" I was genuinely interested, "I mean, I know I can because I have, and for much longer, but I thought you. . ."

"Good Lord," our new resolutions were fighting with her natural tendency to fly off the handle, "has it never entered your weird mind that I want to do it so much because it's you, not because I'm congenitally insatiable?"

"Um, no," I said, unable to stop the gigantic smile filling my face.

"I mean, don't get the wrong idea," she obviously decided that that was enough of being complimentary, "I haven't ever gone that long. It might be good to try, though. It'll be like being a nun."

I suppressed all sorts of rude comments. "I'll get you a

121

habit and a wimple, then," I said, and concentrated on eating while wrestling with half-formed thoughts.

"You see, Liz," I chased some grains of rice round my plate, "I don't want you to feel. . .you know, sort of responsible for me deciding not to go, if I do decide not to go, and put you under pressure to make it work if it turned out that you changed your mind. . ." This time she crossed her eyes, so I tried to pound another idea into submission. "I mean," I groaned, "if I didn't go, it would be mainly because of you, but the idea of the tour's making me think about why I'm in the band, and whether I want to be in it forever, and maybe have to tour even more. . ."

She took pity on me, "So why are you in the band? Apart from for the money, which can't be your main reason, since you're always telling me you're broke."

"I love it," I said on a crest of assurance, "I don't like the travelling so much since you've been here, but I love performing. I'm addicted. There's nothing like that feeling when we get it right, and it takes off, and sometimes. . ." The phone rang.

"I'll get it," Liz stood up and dropped a kiss on the top of my head as she passed. "Oh hi. . .hm. . .hm. . . I see. . .let me just get a pen. . .are you sure you want me to do it, why don't you. . .all right, all right!" I heard her say, and she came back looking frazzled.

"That was Issy again." She sat down and started bolting the rest of her supper, "She wants me to phone Eleanor and advise her to get in touch with Jack. He spun her some tale about Boltons and why he spoke to that stringer, and Issy thinks Eleanor would be interested. She still won't speak to El herself, though, the stubborn thing." She gave me the smile which never failed to ensnare me, "How come we've ended up as piggies in the middle here, how long are we going to have to pass their messages backwards and forwards?"

"Could be ages," I said. "We'll have to charge them for the extra phone calls."

"I can't understand them." She shook her head, "lesbians today, we never carried on like that."

"Issy's got an attack of conscience," I said, "or self-preservation. She doesn't want to get involved with an

Attached Woman."

"Jeez," she put down her fork and stretched out her hand to my leg, "makes me think we're normal."

"Oh darling," I clasped my bosom, "I can't tell you how happy that makes me feel. Have you made a pudding? Jam roly poly? Syrup sponge?"

"Give us a break, woman," she came closer, "when have you given me time this evening to do that kind of thing? I've got a good idea," her hand stopped, "you wash up and I'll phone Eleanor, then we can carry on debating whether we have a future."

"Chloe never made me wash up so much. . .just a minute," I held on to her wrist as a stray thought occurred to me, "talking of exes, how come Pat had Sylv's phone number? She gave it to me on Sunday morning. Did you give it to her? When? Why?"

"What?" She looked confused, then as if she was going to lie, then she laughed.

"Whoops." She tilted her chair on to two legs and balanced for a while before crashing down, "You remember that row we had in the flat over who ate all the chocolate biscuits?"

"No. . ."

"Yes you do. You threw a dictionary at me, and told me to eff off back to Somerset, so I rushed out and nearly killed myself running down the fire escape."

"Didn't I do that every time?" I was back to admiring her ears.

"Yeah, well, this time I decided to go for sure, and I met Ag outside the house and gave her Sylv's number and told her she could always get in touch with me through her. Pat must have tortured Ag to hand it over."

"Why did you decide not to leave?" I didn't realise she'd been so close to going.

"I came back up to get some of my stuff, and you were playing that bloody tune. The one you were playing when I first fell for you."

"Oh yes," I remembered it all now, "and after we made up that night, that was when you took that picture of me playing the fiddle with nothing on."

"Yes."

We looked quietly at each other.

"Kate," she turned my hand over in hers, "I might be being insanely optimistic here, but I think it'll work out between us whatever you decide." She dropped her eyes and studied the lines on my palm, following them with her forefinger. "I know you love playing. I've seen you when you take off, it's when you become who you really are. . .I'm sorry, I'm being cringe-y."

"No," I closed my hand on her fingers, "I've never told anyone this. It's what I was trying to say when Issy rang." I let my eyes open up to hers, "It doesn't happen every time, though when it does, when we really gel and the audience respond, I feel like. . .I feel like I'm taken out of myself, and put in touch with something. . . something bigger and better than me and oh shit, now you'll think I'm loopy."

"No." It was her turn to be deadly serious, "That's what I've seen." She took her hand away and rested her chin on it, so I couldn't see her eyes any more. "I get jealous. I see you and know you're in a place where I'll never be with you." Her back was rigid.

I sat still and prayed I was saying the right thing. "I don't need this band to feel it. I've felt it playing with other people before I joined, and I know I can feel it again without them. But Liz, I feel something similar sometimes when we're, you know, making love, and I don't think I'll get that with anyone else. I haven't so much before, not even with Chloe." She moved her head. "Don't say you're crying on me again," I blinked as I spoke, "I'm the one who's always bursting into tears, remember."

"You're a cow," she blew her nose, "you've ruined my carefree life of fun and casual sex."

"That was always my intention." I snatched her hanky from her, "Call El, then, and I'll lower my artistic sensitive self to wash up."

By Thursday evening, when I stomped through the front door, I was back to normal and furious with Liz. I had arranged to go in our car with Fred to a big hotel in the Lakes where they were planning a midsummer spectacular of music and fireworks, a potentially disastrous event into which Fred had got us embroiled through an acquaintance who had been commissioned to write the music. In a

124

moment of weakness or drunkeness, Fred had agreed to recruit the musicians needed for this ambitious piece, and we were meant to have a planning meeting with the composer and the manager responsible for the overall direction to discuss what was meant to happen and progress so far. I enjoyed sitting in a bay window overlooking a sparkling lake, drinking coffee and eating homemade shortbread, but developed a severe case of brain strain at the thought of the awesome complexity of this entertainment.

"Here's the music," the composer wanged a fat file in my direction. "The first part is ethereal, which is where you come in, doing a haunting melody, and the second part is rowdy with the full ensemble."

"I can do haunting," I said dubiously, casting my eye over his spidery writing. Where did Fred think he was going to find a competent tuba player and a giant gong? My headache got worse when we moved on to discussing a rehearsal schedule, and I realised the whole shebang was only a few weeks away.

"It won't be a problem," Fred said with an excess of confidence. "As long as we can get together for all the day of the performance, with the musicians I have in mind it'll be a doddle."

"Are you really so sure about this?" I asked as we were driving home.

"Of course not, it'll be a dog's dinner right up till the last minute." Fred grinned amiably at me, "Is this car losing power?"

"It shouldn't be. . ." I glanced at the petrol gauge, "The bitch," I pumped impotently at the accelerator and we ground to a halt. "She said the tank was full. I'm coming to the States."

"I won't hold you to that. There was a garage about a mile back. Got a petrol can then, have you?"

"You told me there was petrol in the car!" I shouted at the top of my voice, banging the front door behind me. I knew Liz was in, the radio was on in the kitchen, and I tripped over her boots in the hallway.

"Hm?" She emerged into the sitting room, smiling like the Cheshire cat.

"We had to walk for miles! I hate you, you did this on purpose, don't come near me. . ."

"There was petrol in the car," she folded her arms, "just obviously not enough. You could try looking at the fuel gauge occasionally, and actually paying for some yourself."

"That's so unfair! You use it far more than me, and I paid for the tax and the MOT. . ." We ranted on as usual until my desperate, "Well, you owe me a pound for those strawberries," brought us into each other's arms.

"Thank goodness," she said, her lips still on mine, "it was getting so dull, us being nice to each other all the time. Er," she gently stopped my hand on her second button, "I hate to tell you this, but Eleanor's here. She's stopping for supper."

"What?" I swallowed, took a deep breath and had to smile back, "Now I remember why I never liked you." I released her and raised my voice, "Hi Eleanor."

"Hi Kate," her voice came from the dining area, "good day at the office?"

I went through to find her working on a complicated diagram full of arrows and squiggles.

"Sorry about the shouting. How's it going?" I asked.

"Yeah, well, my domestic life's in ruins and I'm getting spooked and obsessed by this Bradley thing." She threw down her pen, "I've come to consult you and Liz as people I can trust who aren't too involved. I need your opinion."

"Good God," I said, "you must be in a bad way. Have a cup of tea."

"First things first," Eleanor pronounced later, "I've found out that your Jock is a certain Mr McSheady, and he runs this little firm, Borders Security, which is all above board as far as these things go. I've kept what you told me, Liz, about his sideline in booze, under my hat for the time being, in case it comes in handy." She paused and frowned at her diagram before continuing. "I'm just not happy at all about the Bradley set-up and I can smell a big rat somewhere. Amy thinks I'm mad, but I can't let it go." She rushed on, clearly not wanting to digress into her private life, "I've tried to be discreet, in digging and delving, yet I can't help feeling that since I started, someone's trying to keep tabs on me, which is one reason why I'm at Toni's." She glowered at us, as if daring us to suggest otherwise. We kept mum.

"OK," she seemed satisfied that we weren't going to diagnose paranoia or ask her about Amy, "I'll tell you what I know." She cleared her throat and addressed us firmly, like lawyers in a conference.

"The American group, Dexter Holdings, which owns Boltons and Bradleys, started up in food processing, and that's why they acquired Boltons, but they have a property development arm in the States, and have been trying to expand that over here, so they swallowed up Bradleys, which was an obscure Manchester property firm. I get the vague idea," she furrowed her brow, "that they like to get hold of ailing food manufacturing businesses on good sites at knock down prices, and if the factories carry on losing money, they still have the land for development. There was some hoo-ha in the States, and I think they've been investigated on a couple of occasions. Anyway," she pursed her lips, "I couldn't understand why Bradleys haven't started work on the site here. They've got the planning permission and the camp really isn't an issue as far as they're concerned. Then I got lucky, when I spoke to an engineer who works for the building contractors. He's quite a reasonable guy, and we'd set up an informal meeting to discuss whether the hotheads in the BAG camp could be persuaded not to interfere with the work once it had started, and what would happen if they lay down in front of the bulldozers and things like that. But at the end, he let it slip that it all might be hypothetical because Bradleys hadn't come up with the initial payment his firm were demanding, and they were all getting naffed off. Then he shut up and rushed off."

I wasn't making much headway with all of this. "Isn't that good news?" I asked confusedly, "maybe they've just run out of money."

"I wouldn't have thought so," Eleanor tapped the table with her diagram, "I mean, I'm not into the financial side of things, but I would've thought they'd have all the investors and loans set up well before now. And then yesterday, I spoke to Issy's neighbour, Jack." She stopped and tugged at her hair, "The trouble is, I don't know if this is a load of cobblers or if I'm on to something. Jack said," she paused then plunged on, "Jack said he'd wanted to speak to a reporter because an acquaintance of his, an accountant who used to work for Boltons and is now retired, hinted that some time ago, money was moved from Boltons' pension fund into a Bradleys account to make it look like they had more capital; but then the Boltons management got antsy and demanded the money back in case their auditors noticed, and that's why Bradleys have a cash-flow problem."

I was lost. "I'm lost," I said.

Eleanor smiled, "So am I, really. I don't know enough about this kind of thing, and it could easily be an unfounded rumour. I mean, accounting's so complicated, especially in these big corporations, it would be beyond me to find out if they've done anything dodgy or illegal. There wouldn't be anything surprising in Boltons cross-subsidising Bradleys, since they're all part of the same outfit, and if they've been doing that, it could explain why they don't seem to have been doing so well this year."

Liz saw my mouth open and kicked my ankle, "It would be illegal to use a pension fund for anything else," she explained patronisingly, "you should know that."

"Poop to you," I said and concentrated on Eleanor. "So, really, you need to speak to Jack's friend, then you can judge for yourself a bit better."

"Mm," she said thoughtfully, "I'd like to meet him face to face. Now he's retired, though, he lives in Fife."

"I'm going in that direction next week," I said in surprise, "Wednesday night in Edinburgh, Thursday Kirkcaldy, oh joy, and Friday night in Dundee. Back for Saturday lunchtime to play a fun session at the arts centre."

"I was going to go up in the car on Thursday evening to join her," Liz said, an announcement which was news to me. "If you arranged to meet him on the Friday, you could come up with me and get a lift back with us both after the gig on Friday night."

"Do you mind?" Eleanor's face lifted, "It would be good to get away. . ."

"Not at all." Liz smiled, "It'll be a change for me to have some civilised company for once while I chase around the country after Kate."

"OK, I'll see if I can get his address and check it's feasible," Eleanor said. "If you're sure you two won't want to be alone on the way back. . ."

"God no," I said, "I've had enough of this getting along well business. I'll see if there's a space for you in our hotel for the Thursday night, I will draw the line at you sharing our room."

"I don't know," Liz showed her teeth, "a threesome might be just what Eleanor needs. . . aaagh!" She put her arms up against the handful of peanuts I showered her way, "OK, ok, I'll respect your desire to avoid experimentation. . ."

14

"It's ok that Eleanor came up with me, isn't it?" Liz asked after the gig on Thursday night.

"Sure." I moved slightly under her comfortable weight in the warm cocoon of our squeaky hotel bed and gave a happy sigh, "Mmmm. . .Did she say anything about Amy or Issy on the way up?"

"You dreadful gossip." We kissed some more.

"She did say something, didn't she?" I made my hand rest at the base of her spine.

She gave a half-groan, half-giggle, "All right, she did let it drop that she envied us. Don't torment me."

I started retracing the known yet always absorbing map of her curves, "Why should she do that?"

"Why do you think?" Her mouth was like velvet on my skin, "Because she knows we have a lot of fun. God, I want to be doing this still when I'm an old lady. In fact," her hips opened at the brush of my fingertips on her, "this is how I'd like to die."

"Hell. Warn me if you feel a heart attack coming on. . .I wish we had some oil for this bed." I felt that I was about to jump off a cliff into a layer of solid white fluffy clouds.

"There's some in the car. D'you want to go and get it?"

"As if." I arched and jumped and was lost.

The next morning, I sat with Eleanor in the small hotel lobby, giving her surreptitious looks from under my hair. I had decided to join their jaunt out into the country, and now we were waiting for Liz, who was engaged in some engrossing conversation with Fred and Jo over the wreckage of the breakfast table. Eleanor didn't appear to be consumed by jealousy, on the contrary, she was much more affable than she had been when she turned up, weary and pale, with Liz at the gig the previous night. However, her efforts to conceal her astonishment at the amount of food we had just stuffed down had not escaped me.

"It won't make you late for anything, coming with us to see Mr Jess, will it?" Mr Jess was Jack's retired accountant friend, and Eleanor had an eleven o'clock appointment with him.

"Nah." I stretched my legs, almost purring at the sensation brought about by a combination of lovely sex, a full stomach, sunlight beaming through the windows and the prospect of a relaxing day ahead, topped by a gig sharing the bill with the most popular local band. We had taken up the kind offer of a house belonging to a friend of Fred and Jo's for the day. I had the address and a rough map of how to get there stuffed in my pocket, and I was sure Liz and I would manage to sneak off for a snooze in a spare room in the afternoon.

"Kate," Eleanor's voice intruded upon my self-satisfied reverie, "d'you mind if I ask, how did you know for definite that you and Chloe were finished?"

"I think the fact that we'd not got it together for months and had both slept with other people was a pretty strong indication," I said, a bit more acidly than I should have. "Sorry," I flustered, seeing the disappointment on her face, "my mind was elsewhere." I tried to be more open and truthful, "I suppose I really had an inkling when I started finding other women attractive, and I should have known when I actually acted on that for the first time. But it took Chloe sleeping with someone else for it to sink in properly." I'd forgotten that not many people knew about my flings, and had to put up with facing her goggle-eyed surprise and then disapproval.

"You mean, you slept with other women?" she said in a high-pitched whisper. "But you were so upset when Chloe went off with that cosmic bucket therapist or whatever she was. You cried for ever."

"I know," I mumbled, sinking back into my chair. "Not very edifying, is it?" I pulled out a curl and pinged it back to aid putting my addled thoughts into words, "I think it was one thing to give into temptation and tell myself they were meaningless one night stands, and another to realise that we were through. I mean," I cast my mind back, "Chloe and I weren't getting on very well, and we hadn't, you know, done it, for ages, but it was still horrible to know for sure that she didn't want me any more. And you just get used to being in a couple, and having someone there for you all the time, and it was hell to be on my own again after assuming we'd be together for ever and," I warmed to my theme, "there's all the awful practical things on top of everything else, like telling family and sorting out money and possessions and houses. . ." I stopped when I saw her expression sink into moroseness, "Though I'm glad now it all happened," I gabbled, "otherwise I would have never met Liz, and had this. . ."

"Triumph of hope over experience?" she finished for me, and we both laughed.

"Oh dear," I said, "I don't mean to pry, but if what happened to me and Chloe sounds like what you and Amy are going through, then I'd bail out, however difficult it is, and if you're feeling something for Issy. . ."

"Damn," she interrupted, "I am. It's driving me mad, and I find myself wondering if all this paranoia about Bradleys is just a symptom that I'm cracking up in a mid-life crisis." She groaned, "It's a crock of shit, isn't it? Amy and I have been together since law school, we've even discussed where we're going to live when we retire. I'm totally fed up with her, and can't imagine life without her all at the same time. . . anyway," she lifted her head, "here comes the sex goddess, looks like we're off."

I looked up to see Liz loping towards us. Eleanor nudged me, "Don't tell her we call her that, she already knows how fanciable she is. Don't want her getting big-headed."

"What do you call me?" I asked curiously, "The Blob?"

"Only nice things." She was laughing again, "You know we rejoice in your good fortune."

"Ha." I stood up and returned Liz's lazy grin, "Ready to go at last?"

"Yes, oh woman of my dreams." Heavens, she was in a good mood. "Got your handbag?"

"D'you know where we're going?" I asked, settling down on the back seat among the bags and general rubbish.

"Sort of." Eleanor flipped through our battered road atlas, "If I can find the right page. . .it would be easier if they weren't all stuck together, what have you done to it?" It had been at the wrong end of a flask in an argument over a boiled sweet.

"Liz threw coffee over it in a fit of pique," I lied. Liz's eyes, shaded by her sunglasses, held mine in the rearview mirror, and we exchanged complicit smiles.

"I'm not going to make an issue of it," Liz said, doing her favourite impression of an annoying counsellor, "but when you're ready, you'll be able to take responsibility for your actions, instead of trying to pin the blame on other people. . . stop that! I'm trying to drive here."

I removed my hands from around her neck and sat back, grinning mindlessly. Once out of town, we followed Eleanor's precise directions through the clean spare countryside fixed like a storybook illustration under a huge sky, with the North Sea winking into haze in the distance. Apart from giving instructions, Eleanor was silent, as if marshalling her faculties for dealing with Mr Jess, and I gave myself up to reclining in a bubble of good fortune, underpinned by Liz's low humming as she drove.

"This should be it." Eleanor put the atlas down and gave her slim document case a nervous pat, "That cottage on the right. . .yes, Strathburn Mills. . .come in with me won't you? Just to check he isn't a weirdo, then you can go for a tootle or something and come and pick me up later. . ."

We parked on the tidy drive, and piled out to meet the tall figure coming out of his greenhouse. I made the snap architectural judgement that the house had originally been two of those low-walled Scottish agricultural cottages which had been tastefully knocked together to create an eminently desirable retreat, set back from the quiet road with a view over fields and walls to the sea.

"My, quite a committee," the man said, dusting his hand on the seat of his tweedy trousers and holding it out, "I'm Donald Jess." I had expected a wizened old codger, a bit like

Jack, but Donald was a vigorous-looking body, with a ruddy face and dreadfully healthy, though peculiarly detached, eyes. He seemed like the type who'd think nothing of spending his retirement hiking over obscure mountains and moors, drinking from streams and carrying only a handful of raisins and a sturdy stick. We introduced ourselves, and Liz and I made "we'll make ourselves scarce" noises.

"There's a very pleasant walk down to the cliffs, bit of a scramble in places," Mr Jess said, confirming my unfounded surmises. "Though you can stay in the garden if you prefer, while we talk business. I'll show you the kitchen, and you can help yourself to tea and coffee or whatever," his x-ray vision had penetrated to my smokers's lungs and untoned muscles. For a horrible moment, I thought Liz was going to turn hearty on me and express an interest in rambling. Then she picked up my radiating hostility to that type of exertion, switched on the charm, and implied that coffee in his garden would be the most delightful experience.

I left her to assist with the elevenses and wandered to an artfully situated bench round the other side of the house, where I could sit in the sun, look at the sea and eye up the neatly ridged potato patch. Like an angel of plenty, Liz eventually appeared with a tray of coffee, and we sat, faces turned towards the warmth, murmuring niceties to each other, conveniently forgetting Eleanor and the concerns which had brought us here.

"Would be nice to live in the country one day, don't you think?" Liz said, shrugging off her jacket. "You could have that vegetable garden you're always on about with herbs and things, and I could swan around picking roses and making jam."

"In a floaty dress," I said, idly looking at her winter pale arms and the outline of her breasts under her tee shirt. "We could have cats and join the WI and be known as those rather odd but very pleasant ladies at 'Dunboozin'. We'd need to commit a daring bank raid first to get the funds for our dream house, and we would be clothed in an aura of mystery ever after."

"Hm, yerss," she said, and I unwillingly realised that she wanted to tell me something.

"Oh dear," I said, "you haven't already done that, have you?"

"Not recently," she moved her arm along the back of the bench and patted my shoulder. "Don't be alarmed. You looked so seductive a minute ago. No," she squinted up at the sun again, "I had a talk with Ben yesterday. He's been banging on about this for weeks, but he wants me to go into partnership with him. I've still got some money stashed away from when I sold my flat, and he wants me to put that into the business so we can tart up the premises and buy some more equipment, then I can work full time with him, and maybe start earning a decent wage again." She watched my brain cells attempt to process this new information. "I've talked to Eleanor about it, and she'll help me on the legal side, to make sure we have a proper watertight deal, and he's an ok guy really. I think I could work with him."

"That's good, isn't it?" I felt my way blindly, "If that's what you want. . ."

"Yeah, well," her fingers tried to reassure me again, "the downside is that I wouldn't be able to come away with you like this so much. The upside is that I'd be settled, the money could be good and. . ." she rushed out this last bit, "I could think about another mortgage in a bit. A house for both of us, of course. Um. . .I mean, if you didn't fiddle your taxes for a year or so, and showed your true income, we could even consider. . ."

It would have been less of a shock if she had ripped off her clothes and pranced singing merrily towards the sea. "A joint mortgage?" I said, sounding like a crackly recording of the last castrati in the Vatican choir.

"You're probably an appalling risk, but yeah, perhaps it's something we could think about."

Struck dumb, I let it sink in that this was the closest to a marriage proposal I'd ever get. A butterfly flickered on some early bloom, and I felt the earth tilt and tectonic plates move inside me.

"Don't get too carried away," Liz's voice was as mild as the breeze on my face, "there's a big complication." I saw the spark under the amusement in her eyes.

"Huuurgh, what?" Any more of this, and I would dissolve into a pool of melted butter.

"You know I was talking to Fred and Jo?"

"Guh," I nodded.

"They basically said that they'd been doing their sums with the money you've been offered for the States thing. It's being sponsored by a bunch of arts organisations, so there's a fair bit sloshing around, and they think the organisers have budgeted for a sound engineer cum roadie cum jack of all trades with you. So. . .so they asked me. The others are cool with it, if you agree. What d'you think? Would you like me to come?"

Once, when my younger brother and I were small, my parents had taken it into their heads that a long family walk would be just the thing to stop us spending a summer Sunday fighting and demanding ice lollies every fifteen minutes. They had packed us into the car and driven for miles to some hill in the Welsh borders, then dragged us whingeing and whining to the top. A bundle of resentment, I had looked under instruction at the view, the still valley below and the folded mountains rolling to beyond the limits of my imagination, and in an incomprehensible rush, I had known the world to be an enchanted playground, full of unexplored delights which one day would be mine. Sliding along Mr Jess's bench and putting my mouth to Liz's for a kiss which reached my toenails, I was back on that hill and flying like a lark into the sun.

"I'll take that as a yes, then." Liz rested her forehead against mine, "Better not get too passionate, there's probably a law against this in Scotland."

"Huuuuh," the ability to form words had temporarily eluded me.

"I know, I'll have to put any plans with Ben on hold, and he might not want to wait until next autumn. Or maybe I'll just take six months off unpaid and dump him in it." She extricated herself and reached for the coffee pot, "Have a refill, you look like you need one. Maybe you'd better have a cigarette as well."

I rolled probably the most misshapen cigarette I have ever tried to smoke, and wobbled my lighter towards it. "But. . ."

"I know," she repeated patiently, "we'll have to think about it a bit more carefully. I'll have to really learn how to work the sound deck and stuff, and it'll be a real test to see if we're suited. I mean," she took the cigarette and had a drag herself, "I complain that you're away and everything, but it works quite well, we have space away from each other, and it's fantastic when we get together and can spend all day in bed. It'll be different if we're in each other's hair twenty four hours a day for six months with a load of other people, travelling and trying to work together and getting ratty and tired and not having much privacy. We might end up hating each other."

"I'm prepared to chance it," I took the cigarette back, "Fred and Jo have managed for years. And anyway, we'll probably have slowed down by next year and be a bit more sedate. The pebbles in the jar and all that."

"The what?" For a moment she looked as if she was regretting taking on a madwoman.

"You know," I grinned at her, "that old wives' tale. You put a pebble in a jar for every time you do it in your first year together, and after your first anniversary, you start taking one out every time you do it, and the jar never gets empty."

"God, you're a mine of dispiriting information. I wish you hadn't told me that." She rested her eyes gloomily on a spindly clematis in an oversized planter and perked up, "Still, we'd probably need a jar that size, the rate we're going."

"And some of the pebbles would have to be boulders," I stubbed out the cigarette.

She put down her mug and stood up, "Um. . .let's go for a little walk. I've got to spend this afternoon having a lesson on electronics with Dave. . ."

When we returned, Eleanor and Mr Jess were standing a few feet apart in front of the bench, holding a stilted conversation.

"Here they are," Eleanor's relief was patent, "we'll be off then. Thank you for your time, Mr Jess, I won't be bothering you again, I hope."

He looked at us, "So you went for a walk after all. Did you get to the cliffs?"

"Not quite," I gushed, "but it's such beautiful countryside here." Countryside with which, I didn't say, I was far more intimately acquainted than I had been a couple of hours previously. I laid it on with a trowel, "And thank you for the coffee, it was so kind of you."

He smirked, "You're welcome, have a pleasant trip back." We all shook hands again and made for the car.

"Where the fuck've you been? And why is your hair full of leaves, Kate? Honestly, I can't believe you two. . ." Eleanor said, clearly feeling the strain.

"Sorry," Liz was unrepentant, "just communing with nature."

"Nature my arse." Eleanor wrenched the passenger door open, "It's a nightmare being around you both when I'm in this state. I think I'll have to find where the action is tonight and pick someone up."

"Just as long as you're back with us at midnight, or you'll miss your lift back," I said temperately, trying to clean out my hair with the aid of the wing mirror.

"That's more than enough time, don't worry," Eleanor started to laugh, "I'm sorry, it was heavy going in there. He's a tough nut all right."

I flopped into the back again, and we set off.

"Didn't you get what you wanted, then?" Liz asked, turning out on to the road.

I leaned forward to dab at the streak of earth on the back of her shirt.

"Well, I did eventually. He's odd, I think he's basically unscrupulous. He more or less confirmed what Jack said, but I think he sees accounting as some abstract game with no implications in the real world. I get the feeling he was reluctant to tell me about it because he couldn't quite grasp why I should be interested, more than because his bosses broke the law. It's like he didn't make the connection between these sums of money floating around from account to account in some sort of banking cyberspace, and the destruction of a patch of countryside. It was almost as if he's very slightly. . . autistic, even. Like he's learned how to behave socially, but that isn't where he's really at. Still, he copied a load of disks for me, and said the details are all on them. My guess is that he kept them because they remind him of how clever he is, and he told Jack just to show off."

"What're you going to do, then?" Liz asked, "Blackmail Bradleys and demand a pay-off?"

I tutted self-righteously behind her.

"There's a possibility," Eleanor's good temper had reasserted itself. "No, I'll probably take the disks to someone who can make sense of them, and if we've got a case, we can take it from there. . . I'd turn left here, if we're going to Dundee. I wonder what the scene's like there."

The rest of the day reminded me of Christmas Eve. We found Fred and Jo's friend's house, in a salubrious area alongside the Tay. Liz went off with Dave, while Eleanor disappeared on an errand of her own. I spent the afternoon dozing in an armchair. All the time, drifting in and out of sleep, the knowledge of my luck ran incandescent through my veins. I could have the band *and* Liz. What more could I want, I would be a nicer person from now on and never complain about anything ever again.

The others seemed perfectly adjusted to the idea of Liz joining the tour, and included her in our chatter backstage over an Indian take-away after the gig.

"We're going to build you a collapsible sound-proof room," Bill said to me backstage after the gig, his mouth full of nan bread, "so you can erect it, as it were, where you will, and have your own little world."

"Now Liz," I could hear Dave saying on the other side of our makeshift table, "would you be up for doing the sound at our regular spots in the Billhook from now on? The boys there won't mind, and it'll be good practice."

"Sure." She passed a foil dish to Eleanor, who had joined us after all, "And Kate and I did sit down and work out the dates I could join you on this year's tour. I could learn a lot from those as well."

Oh my, I thought, cue theme music and roll the titles, I can't stand feeling so good, and I'm not going to spoil this biryani by crying into it. I hid my face behind a chapatti.

With Eleanor to help, we packed up the van in record time, and waved the others off as Fred shouted instructions to be at the arts centre at one o'clock sharp the next day. Then Liz, Eleanor and I had a committee meeting and my view, that I should drive because I'd had some sleep that day, prevailed, mostly as a result of Eleanor's casting vote, although I swore a solemn oath that I would pull over if I felt my eyelids so much as blink. We shot back over the Tay, intoning our own version of the Tay Bridge Rail Disaster, and since no-one seemed inclined to sleep, fell to exchanging girlie confidences in the closed cosiness of the car.

"I'm beginning to think," Eleanor pronounced from the back after we had run through first crushes, experiences with men and who we would rather be shot than have to sleep with, "that I never forgave Amy."

"For what?" I said, wondering if the car behind us was going to overtake or spend all night up our backside.

"Sleeping with Bel, of course." She sounded almost ashamed.

"But I thought you had. I mean, you've stayed together, and it's only recently that you've started thinking it might be over," I sighed with relief as the distracting car pulled out and roared off.

"Yeah, I thought I had. I mean, I loved her, and it was really good again once Bel had left, and I thought we'd worked it out and it didn't matter. And then she was quite upset the night I was moving out to Toni's and," her voice faltered, "I can't quite believe I did this, but I turned round and told her it was all her fault for going off with Bel. It just popped out without me thinking. I mean, how childish can you get, it was years ago."

"I dunno," Liz piped up, "there's no telling how these things affect you. I bet if I met up with Mags, my first serious girlfriend, I could still find it in me to be cross with her for going off with someone else. Keep your eyes on the road, my love, it's kind of an essential part of the driving experience."

"Really?" I said, not taking offence, "But you've had so many. . . partners since."

"Not that many. . . all right," she prised my pincer-like grip from above her knee and put my hand back to the steering wheel, "I have slept with loads of women. I suppose I believed that there were lots of beautiful women out there, and I wanted to experience as many and as much as possible. And when we were at college we were all into that not conforming with the patriarchal system and not trying to imitate straight couples and be restricted by outdated notions of monogamy. . . are you sure you're ok driving, Kate, you didn't have a drink back there, did you?"

"No," I gripped the wheel more firmly, "I just didn't know you were so. . . intellectual and sorted about it."

"Well, I thought I was. I did have a lot of nice times, and I can't honestly say I regret any of it. It's only that I think I've discovered, rather late in life I admit, how strong jealousy is, and how it can really do your head and everything else in." Her hand went to my thigh.

139

"Can I take that as a compliment?" I made sure I was staring at the road.

"I think you can."

"Oh Lord," Eleanor said testily, "stop the car if you're going to make out. And next time, make sure you don't have big slurpy kisses in front of a window where I can see you."

15

Later, Liz and Eleanor did fall asleep and, buoyed up by happiness, I drove carefully on through the night. Having decided that negotiating my way on to the Forth Road Bridge and along the slower road south through Biggar would be more likely to keep me awake, I didn't catch up with the van. At some point near Carlisle, when I'd hit the motorway, Liz stirred beside me and lifted her head from the bundled up sweater she was using as a pillow.

"You ok still?" she mumbled, her eyes not even half open.

"Yeah, go back to sleep, sweetie," I whispered, aware of some new gentleness in my voice.

"You're a darling," she shut her eyes again, and I concentrated fiercely on the road. Of course, I then found that I was dying for a pee, and they both woke up properly when I swung into the all-night services and lurched into a parking space. Frowsty and stiff, we plumped for having a coffee as well, and with Liz driving, rejoined the motorway in an artificial burst of pre-dawn energy.

"Got any music?" Eleanor asked, "Something to sing along to?"

I clacked through the tapes lying around in the front, found some bizarre compilation I'd put together years before, and turned it up loud. Spurred on by our less than tuneful accompaniment, Liz drove far too fast, and about an hour later we belted off the motorway and past the Lodge Hotel, bellowing along to "Don't leave me this way." Stuck in high-pitched mode, I didn't take much notice of the car which pulled out of the hotel entrance and fell in close behind us.

"Good timing," Liz commented, glancing at the dashboard clock when the track came to its end, and we were bowling towards Toni's street along a popular rat run by some playing fields, "be able to get some sleep in before I go to take wedding pictures and Kate has to be at the arts centre. Got a key for Toni's, El? All right if we just drop you off. . . Fucking hell!" She slammed on the brakes with all her force, I threw my arms up to my face and Eleanor screamed as an unlit transit van shot out of a side street and stopped broadside in the road, blocking our way. We skidded to a halt inches away from its grimy bodywork.

"You fuck," Liz undid her seatbelt and kicked her door open, propelling herself like a vengeful arrow at the driver of the van, who was jumping down from his seat, the fluorescent bars on his jacket flashing in our headlights. I saw her fists clench and fury spring along her body. Too shaken to ask Eleanor if she was all right, I hauled myself out of the car towards Liz, with only the thought that I would help her strangle the driver. A car drew up behind ours, and I opened my mouth to add my contribution to Liz's stream of abuse. Then an iron bar clamped round my ribs and bile-tasting air whooshed out of my mouth. From outer blackness, I heard Eleanor cry out again, my arm was wrenched behind my back as if by a force of nature, and a hard claw took me by the back of the neck and flung me against the side of the van.

"Got you, you bitch," a male voice, accompanied by a breath of foul air, battered my ear drums. I knew it was the security guard from the Bradley site. I felt his weight pressing into my back, and in a hysteria of pain and helpless terror, tried to kick out at him, cries and sounds from around me tumbling senselessly into my floundering.

"Kate, Kate. . .get off me, you bastard. . ." I think that was Liz, though I didn't really recognise her voice. A car door slammed. Bob Marley was giving it his all on the next track. My free hand met nothing except unyielding clothing.

"Let them both go, I'm going to wake the city," Eleanor's shout ended in a blast of our car horn which stopped suddenly as if her hand had been cut off. The music died.

"Och, calm down everybody," the unruffled smooth command rose above the confusion, and I stopped struggling.

"Jock," Liz's voice fell like a spent bullet. I still couldn't see her.

"Ms Sharpe, you do get around don't you? Stop trying to molest my employee, he's a family man. Besides, the young chappie who fancies your musical friend is in the unfortunate habit of carrying a stanley knife with him. We'll all do as I say, and then there'll be no accidents to her hands. I hear it's no' easy to play a violin with severed tendons."

If I lived to be a hundred and two, I never wanted to hear Liz make a noise like that again. I still couldn't help it. With all the conditioning of adulthood gone, I retched and whimpered against the van's cold metal side, "Do it, do as he says, please." I could smell the young man's sweat, and retched again.

"That's better." Jock sounded happy, "This is what's going to happen. Ms Sharpe, you and Ms Knighton, our nosy legal friend, are going to accompany me and my driver in my car. I hope you understand that this is only an invitation to a business meeting, nothing to get over-excited about." The tension in the quiet street dropped a millimetre or two. He went on, "As a wee precaution, though, I think your curly-topped girlfriend should travel in the van with my other two bonny lads. We've all got mobiles, to aid communication so to speak, isn't technology a wonderful thing? So, any hanky panky from you girls and oops, a sad loss to the world of music."

It sank in. Liz cried out again, a knife twisting in my heart, penetrating even beyond my fear.

"It's ok." I tried to send my words to her unseen figure, "It's ok, just do as he says, I'm ok."

"We haven't got all night," Jock's tone was clipped, "let's go."

I was pulled away from the van and shoved to the rear doors. I wriggled desperately and at last saw Liz, making a futile lunge towards me until the van driver's armlock forced her to stand still. In the vehicle lights, I could see the broken despair on her face, and it was almost a relief to be pushed up into the back of the van and released to slump down against a wheel arch, the doors clanging shut behind me. I brought my knees up, huddled my arms around them and buried my face in my thighs. If I only focussed on keeping breathing, I would be all right. I heard the front doors open and the driver and his mate get in. I started to shake.

"There's some sacks in there somewhere." This must have been the driver's voice, "You can make yourself a bit more comfortable." He sounded northern and ordinary, "Want a smoke?"

I looked up at the middle-aged back of his neck and nearly burst into tears at this almost normal exchange. I was about to be pathetic enough to take the cigarette he was holding over his shoulder, when I realised I had my tobacco and lighter in my jacket pocket. Thank God I'd put it on when we stopped at the services, and not taken it off again.

"Got my own," I whispered, and sent the strongest messages I could to my fingers to stop jumping around and roll the tobacco properly. The driver grunted, did a bit of competent reversing and turning, and off we went.

"Oooh, get her," the obnoxious security guard craned round to look at me, "proper little butch with her roll-ups. Hate men then, do you? Never had a proper one, that's why, should get me to join you and your girlfriend, tell me what you do, and I'll improve on it, do you. . ."

His filthy suggestions covered me like sewage, and I stared as if meditating at the glowing end of my cigarette. When I'd finished it, I put my hands over my ears and my face back down, and above the sick pulsing of my guts, played Beethoven's violin concerto to myself in my head. I had the music in the house somewhere, and tomorrow I would find it and start practising it again. I remembered my brother and I murdering it when we were teenagers to make my dad laugh, with my brother on the piano pretending to be a Russian concert pianist, tossing his head, and falling off the stool at the end. I would phone him tomorrow as well. It was ages since I'd seen my nieces. They would like Liz, she could take some nice photos of them for my mum. . . I was crying into the privacy of my knees.

"Give it a rest, Carl." I realised the van driver was growling at his companion, "We're here to do what the man says. No need to make it worse."

Carl laughed, "You'd fucking like to do it as well. What's wrong, bothered about what the wife. . . " I sensed the driver stiffen and Carl turned sulky, "Ah, forget it, just a bit of fun."

"Shut it," the driver said conversationally, "I'd like a bit of peace and quiet for a change."

I smeared my tears with my sleeve, and risked a look out of the front windscreen. It wasn't exactly getting light yet, but I could see we were heading north on the old main road, following a pair of red tail lights. Liz and Eleanor. As long as I was going to the same place as them, it would be fine. . . I rolled another cigarette and made my mind a blank apart from an image of Liz's face smiling at me as we boarded a plane for the States. The countryside became dark grey rather than black, and we passed the trackway down which Liz and I had been adventurous in the car. Comprehension dawned along with the morning, and I was hardly surprised when we skirted Kirktown, sped along the coast road, turned off more slowly into Seacliffe and finally scrunched up the drive to Bolton House. We parked round the back in what had once been an elegant stable yard, and an electronic gate swung shut behind us.

"OK?" The driver glanced round at me, "Sorry it was a bit long in the back there. Right," he looked at Carl, "get out and check where we're taking them. I'll make sure she doesn't run away."

I had another spasm of fear. He wasn't nice at all, he was just fooling me and would attack once he had me to himself . . . the back doors of the van opened, and I found myself shrinking back into the wheel arch.

"Come on," he sounded awkward, "I think they want you inside."

I made myself get to my feet, stagger to the door and step out without taking his proferred hand. I looked about wildly. There was Jock, studying his watch and saying something to Carl and the other driver; there was Eleanor, running her hands through her hair; and there, staring towards the van, was Liz. She saw me and we flew together.

"Oh Christ, oh Christ," her heart was racing and her voice was ragged, "Kate, Kate, oh Christ."

"It's all right," I held her as tight as I could, "I'm all right."

"Your hands, did they. . .?"

I took one hand from her back and wiggled it in front of her face, "All present and correct." Now I was in her arms, nothing terrible could happen to me.

She buried her face in my neck, "All the way here. . .that fucker Jock kept saying. . .they might do it anyway, just for fun. . .I couldn't bear. . ." I rubbed my cheek against hers, and felt her heart bump again, "They didn't. . . they didn't do anything else to you. . .?" The question was sticking in her throat.

I drew back slightly and smiled into the twin black wells of her eyes, "Nah. That wanky security man, Carl, gave me a load of verbal abuse, but. . . "

"What?" Her fingers gripped convulsively at the back of my clothes under my jacket.

"Oh sweetheart, just the usual man stuff. I can't say I enjoyed it, but he didn't do anything."

"I'll get him. I swear to God, I'll get him." The certainty in her words was like an epitaph.

"Liz. . ."

"Break it up, you two, you're coming inside," Jock's raised voice made me cling harder to her. He shouted louder, "Come on!", and I cravenly broke away to start walking, holding Liz's hand.

"I'm sorry," Eleanor whispered as we were herded through a back door, "if I'd thought this would happen. . ."

"'S'ok," I stretched out my free hand to touch her elbow, "you weren't to know."

We were led through a characterless corridor to a flight of back stairs, and through a modern fire door into a carpeted passageway, vestiges of the house's former graciousness still clinging to its high ceiling and moulded cornices.

"In here," Jock opened a heavy panelled door, and we filed in. The incongruity of our capture hit me as I took stock of our surroundings. We were in some kind of conference room, furnished with a long gleaming table and reasonably comfortable looking chairs. A flip chart, still covered with the words "targetting resources", "maximising potential" and "motivating the individual", stood at one end of the room, and next to it an overhead projector crouched like the skeleton of some small long-dead dinosaur on a metal trolley. At the other end of the room was a door marked "Bathroom". Lovely, we could all have another pee. Automatically, I walked to the tall sashed windows, and looked out on a stretch of lawn ending in a wall of trees. This must be the back of the house, Sherlock, I said to myself, otherwise you'd be able to see the drive.

"OK ladies," Jock had the air of a man whose mission has been accomplished, "I'm afraid the others are a bit late, not to worry, they'll be along soon. You stay here," he pointed at the van driver, "make sure they don't jump out of the windows, and you two," he wagged his finger at Carl and the other driver, "front and back door. Be nice and polite to any stray callers, and check that they piss off sharpish. I'll be in the main office, give us a bell if you've any problems." He clapped his hands once, "The windows are locked by the way, and don't be tempted to smash them and start screaming. Carl and his wee knife won't be far away." He and Carl smiled like boys about to pull the wings off flies, and swaggered out with the other driver.

"I blame the movies myself," Eleanor said suddenly into the clean space left by their departure. "Too many films about supposed hard men. Gives these people stuck in adolescence funny ideas. Right," she was ignoring the van driver, "goody, goody, a coffee machine. Let's see if we can make a brew and start sorting out our case." The three of us looked at her with our mouths open. She continued blithely, "It'll be a cracker. Assault, kidnap, driving in a manner likely to cause an accident. . ."

"Psychological torment," I cottoned on, "could we go for substantial damages in a private prosecution as well?" I went to the coffee machine on a side table in front of a window, and found ample cheering supplies of coffee, sugar, UHT milk and. . . "Biscuits!" I said, waving the little packet of three in the air. If I pretended this kind of thing happened to me every day, then we would all be safe. I picked up the glass coffee jug and made for the bathroom door, "I'm just going to get some water," I said in the vague direction of the driver, "but if I don't come out in about five minutes, you can assume I've gone out the window and down the drainpipe." Actually, it had occurred to me that this might be a possibility, since my exhausted and overstretched brain was now yelling at me that I had to be at the arts centre at one o'clock, and all this was going to make me late. Once I had snuck into the small room containing a sink and a loo and climbed on to the sink to open the tiny frosted window, however, I realised that no power on earth would be able to propel me up and out through that narrow gap.

I returned with my full jug, set the machine off and sat next to Liz, who was slumped at the table, her head bowed. Eleanor produced a pen from her pocket, ripped a clean piece of paper from the flip chart and sat down opposite us, while the driver, looking wary, plonked himself on a chair he positioned near the door. I would have to think up a plan B.

I put my arm over Liz's shoulders and caught Eleanor's eye. I was startled. I had thought she was putting on an act to keep our spirits up, and to stop us begging for mercy, yet now I saw the huge steely strength fixed like a ramrod in her being. She smiled like a fox in a henhouse, "If they touch your hands, Kate, they're fucked and they know it. They got us frightened and it worked to get us here. McSheady's lot may be a bunch of thugs, but the people they're working for will be more subtle. Don't let them bully us. Try and hold on to the fact that hurting us will only harm them." It was a side of the clever, hardworking, yet funny and loving Eleanor I never knew existed. The coffee machine hiccupped behind me, and Liz gave a great sigh, raising her head.

"You're right, I'm sorry I lost it back there." I could tell how painful it was for her. I was getting more and more ashamed of my abject cowardice as well.

"It's natural. I panicked until my mind kicked in," Eleanor said, doodling on her bit of paper. "We're all very tired. I've seen a lot of people in shock, one way or another, and that's what we've been in." She gave Liz a firm look, "Even the strongest person can't hold out against the fear of seeing someone they love get hurt. The coffee's ready."

Liz produced a wobbly smile and stood up, "I'll get it." She bent her head again, "What about him?" she muttered, flicking her eyebrows towards the driver.

"He can help himself," Eleanor said in her normal clear voice.

"I think he's not that bad," I whispered. I was finding it difficult to behave as if he wasn't there.

"Maybe," Eleanor mouthed back, "but we can play our own games."

We settled down with our coffee and biscuits, and I shut my eyes at the pleasure of having the hot sweet liquid glugging down my throat. I would enjoy this even if I ended up in a concrete overcoat. I extracted my tobacco and lit up.

"Erum." We all jumped at the sound of the previously silent driver clearing his throat. He pointed to a prominent No Smoking sign on the door.

"So, call Carl," I said recklessly, and exhaled vigorously.

"Aw fuck it," he pulled out his own cigarettes, stuck one in his mouth and shambled towards the coffee machine, "I'm not sure I'm getting paid enough for this."

Eleanor clenched her fist and raised it in a gesture of triumph behind his back, "We've got him," she mouthed again, then said casually, "how did you know where we'd be to stop our car?"

"Wasn't hard," he sat down, this time at the table a few seats along from Eleanor, "McSheady seemed to know you were leaving Dundee in the night and would be heading for Alma Street when you turned up." This was the street where Toni lived. "All he had to do was pick you up when you passed the Lodge, and call us so we could block you off at a good spot. Would have been trickier if you hadn't gone by them playing fields. . ." He stopped, as if remembering that we were enemies.

I got up and refilled our cups, puzzling over how on earth Jock had known our movements. Even if someone was keeping tabs on Eleanor, surely no-one would have followed her and Liz all the way up to Scotland, round Fife yesterday . . .

"Donald Jess," Eleanor said in an extraordinary feat of mind-reading. "I wouldn't put it past him to have taken it into his screwed up mind to call his old bosses. I'm afraid I told him you two were friends from home and we we're leaving after you'd played in Dundee that night. When I was trying to make conversation," she added apologetically.

I flexed my hands on the table, and studied them as if I'd never seen them before. What would it be like, I thought, to have all those practised connections I took for granted severed. . . I screamed, "**My violin!** My violin's in the car! What have you. . .?" I looked frantically at the driver.

He managed to stop spitting out his mouthful of coffee, "Bloody hell." He wiped his mouth on his hand, "You've a pair of lungs on you."

He surveyed us slowly. He was an ordinary bloke, thinning hair, smoker's lines on his face and rough, veined hands, and clearly getting more uncomfortable by the second. Whether this was because he was basically decent, or because of the thought that we might possibly live to bring him to justice, I didn't particularly care. I wondered if his wife knew where he was and what he was doing, and thought I heard another car pull into the stable yard.

"Fuck it," he said again, "your car should be all right. We had another lad in the van with us. He was told to hang back, then move the car and park it up somewhere, leave the keys in the wheel arch."

"Park it where?" Eleanor asked, looking puzzled.

"Dunno, to be honest. Should be safe unless some no-good druggie breaks in." A twinge of something like shame twitched in his cheekbones, "It's done on a need to know basis with McSheady. I don't know the half of what goes on, I just do as I'm told. Need the job." His eyes slid away from me and his voice fell, "Sorry, like, about Carl. He's all mouth and no trousers."

"You hurt my arm," Liz's accusation was matter of fact.

"Yeah." He shrugged, "Didn't think you'd be so fucking strong." He took out another cigarette, "Big business eh? The bosses do what they like and we all get fucked and I end up in this heap of shit, fighting women." He breathed out and looked at us again, "I dunno what all this is about really, but if I were you, I'd agree to what they say. They'll win, they always do, and it's best to go along with it, unless you want to end up down the jobcentre or worse. . ." He broke off, stubbled out his cigarette and stood up hastily as the door opened, and Jock led three men, besuited and about as cuddly as hitmen, into the room.

16

My panic returned, and I sat on my hands to conceal their trembling as the three men took seats at the head of the table, putting their briefcases neatly by their chair legs. The driver went back to the door, standing this time, and Jock pulled a chair away from the table to sit by the flip chart. I began thinking of doctors' cases, and metal instruments glinting in the businessmen's banal bags. Eleanor tapped the pen against her teeth and yawned ostentatiously.

"About time," she said as if she was in her office, "we're all busy people."

The three men looked at us indifferently. The bossman in the middle was older and heavier, with a tanned face and eyes used to authority, while the other two were younger versions of corporate man. A faint whiff of aftershave came our way. They could do what they wanted with us, I thought, slipping back into hysteria, five men against three women, and another two outside. . .

"Smile for the camera!" Before I could grasp what she was up to, Liz had taken a tiny camera from her pocket, and was lining up the three men in its sights. She clicked the button rapidly, and popped the camera back into her jacket.

"We'll have that." The big chief spoke matter of factly in an American accent, and made a gesture towards Jock, who got to his feet.

"Aw, don't get your knickers in a twist," Liz drawled. She produced the camera again and tossed it over our heads at Jock, "Got no film in it anyway."

He fumbled the catch, picked the camera up from the floor and tried to open it.

"Little thingy at the top," Liz said helpfully, "it's insured, be as cack-handed as you like."

Jock gave up, and put the camera on the table in front of the boss. I stopped sitting on my hands, and reached for my papers and tobacco.

"There's no smoking in this building," corporate man number one, who was sitting closest to me, said.

I was profoundly grateful for all the times Liz had pushed me to beyond the bounds of reason. "I'll be darned," I said, lighting up, "I've been assaulted, bundled in a van and subjected to vile harrassment all in the same day. I'm not going to give up smoking as well." If Jock comes at me, I thought viciously, I'm going to stub this out on his nose. I drained my coffee cup and flicked ash on the floor, a habit I abominated.

"I don't think," the boss's voice was silky, "that you quite appreciate your situation." He clicked his fingers at corporate man number two, who bent down and opened his briefcase. Fuck, I thought, was that bathroom window really that high up?

The boss continued, "First of all, I will apologise for the unorthodox way in which you were brought here. Meetings are so hard to arrange to everyone's satisfaction, we felt we were justified in resorting to more proactive measures. Secondly," he took what his sidekick was handing him, "this gathering is not taking place, and I see no urgent need to tell you our names." He put a clear plastic folder on the table. "When you returned from Dundee earlier this morning, strangely enough, the three of you didn't go to your homes." He was getting into his stride and clearly relishing it, "Instead you drove to Langdale View, a hotel on River Quay." This was the nearest the city had to a red light district. "In spite of the anti-social hour, you knocked on the door until the proprietor let you in, and you booked into a double room. The three of you." He let that sink in, then I saw the faintest frown darken in his eyes. Liz had snatched Eleanor's pen and paper from her, and was slouched over the table, drawing an elaborate heart with an arrow through it, doing her most irritating low drone at the same time. He powered on, "I have a page of the register you signed, Ms Knighton," he gestured at a lined sheet in the plastic folder, "it's a copy of course. When you departed in, oh, let's say, the late morning, the chambermaid found you'd left a somewhat rumpled bed, and these." As if handling dead beetles, he put a couple of roaches, a scrap of tin foil with some brown substance on it, and what looked like a porn mag on the table. "A good time was had by all, I'd say."

Liz finished writing "Liz'n'Kate" on her heart, and lifted her head. "Give us a look, mate," she said eagerly, and stretched out her hand to the magazine. I slapped her wrist.

"Don't be disgusting," I said snappily, "it's degrading."

"Be ok if it's all women," she whined.

"No." I pushed her hand back, and she subsided grumbling to begin giving herself an ink tattoo on her wrist, breathing noisily through her mouth. She must have been a nightmare at school.

"Shut up," the bossman injected some venom into his voice, and I remembered what used to annoy my teachers. I leaned back and started rocking on the back legs of my chair, letting myself nearly overbalance and then bang into the table. I was at the mercy of a bunch of ruthless men, being fitted up for a drug-fuelled orgy, and I didn't care. Surely only I had seen the message Liz had concealed in the shading of her heart, "Fool around so they just talk to El." She had a plan. I didn't have a clue what it was, but I clung to the thought.

"Ms Knighton," the boss had decided to concentrate on Eleanor, the star of the class, "we're an international corporation. As such, I'm sure you will understand that our primary duty is to our shareholders. They have entrusted us with their investments, sometimes their life savings, and we have to do our utmost to ensure that they receive a fair reward for their trust in us." He sighed sadly, "It's not an ideal world, maybe this is not the best commercial system man could devise, but we have to work within it, and play our part in ensuring we all strive towards the best business practice." He ignored the derisive snort which Liz turned into a sneeze. "But we also see ourselves as having a duty to the wider community, and especially to the local communities in which we operate. Our role as I see it," he started making little gestures with his hands, "is to take the capital we have in our care and to use our expertise to create with it products and services which will enhance people's lives, while at the same time creating opportunity for meaningful employment and the development of skills within our local communities. We are part of a process, Ms Knighton, by which wealth is used, expanded and redistributed as far as possible to the benefit of everyone." By this time, Liz had fallen forward again, and was resting her head on her forearms, looking up at him with one bored eye, and giving muted abstracted groans every now and again. I had picked up the pen, and was tapping out the tripping 7/8 rhythm of one of the eastern European tunes we played in the band and softly whistling its weaving melody over the top. "And you know," the boss leaned ever so slightly towards Eleanor, excluding us with his shoulder, "we are always trying to balance what we would ideally like to do in pursuit of our goals with the concerns of people like your clients, who have justified worries about the environmental costs of the wealth creation necessary to sustain a reasonable life for the people of our small planet. They are entitled to their view, indeed," he became even more sincere, "we need people like that. They keep us on our toes, and remind us to work towards a genuine dialogue, from which cooperation, rather than confrontation, can arise. I have been in business many years," his tone became thoughtful, "and I regret to say that I have sometimes cut corners in my desire to go for what I can see is the greater good. I think you have stumbled upon one of these minor corners. But my conscience doesn't trouble me as much as it would if we had to discontinue operations in this small community, where I know we make a positive contribution to the local economy and hence to the whole social fabric of the area." He clicked his fingers again, and corporate man number two brought out a handful of computer disks. Eleanor's eyes narrowed. "Yes," the boss nodded his head, "I'm afraid McSheady did examine the contents of your document case. I apologise once more." He jerked sharply, and Jock half stood up as Liz rose clumsily to her feet, rocking the table.

"Got to pee," she said drowsily, and tripped over her chair legs on the way to the bathroom. Jock pointed at the driver, who looked dubiously at the bathroom door.

"Come in if you like," Liz said amiably, "I'm sure you've seen it all before."

The driver blushed, and restricted himself to standing by the door, which Liz didn't even bother to shut properly. Above the distinctive noises she was making, I flogged my dozy brain cells to work out what this executive meant by his speechifying. Perhaps all he was saying was that if Eleanor didn't stop interfering, they would close Boltons, making Kirktown a ghost town, and that would be on Eleanor's conscience for the rest of her life. Though how did he propose to persuade us not to kick up a fuss about being kidnapped. . .? There was more commotion as Liz flushed the loo and came back into the room, buttoning up her jeans and giving the table leg a casual buffet in passing. In a burst of insight, I knew the boss was considering sending us both from the room, snapping quickly through the logistics of who could guard us, and where he could put us. He must have decided that this would be more trouble than it was worth, since he waited for Liz to sit down before he renewed his browbeating of Eleanor.

"I'm a reasonable man. . ." he had to stop again, when Liz got to her feet once more and made for the coffee machine. She sniffed at the contents of the jug, and tapped me on the shoulder, doing an elaborate mime to see if I wanted some. I nodded and hissed "Biscuits!", she poured out two new cups, and then we made a lot of satisfying rustles and crunches, scattering sugar packets everywhere and fighting over the one pack of chocolate digestives.

"Settle down!" the boss barked, and we smirked behind our hands.

"I'm a reasonable man," he repeated, "and I think you're a reasonable woman. I believe we could entertain the possibility of coming to an agreement whereby you cease to represent the Bradley Action Group, and see fit not to make any comment on this matter again. I understand that in cases like these, it would be quite acceptable for you to be reimbursed for the legal work you have done so far. There would be nothing unusual in a donation from an anonymous well-wisher being used for such a purpose."

"How much?" Eleanor said, cutting to the chase with admirable swiftness.

He took a gold-capped pen and a black notebook from his pocket, tore out a page, wrote down a figure, folded it up and passed it to Eleanor. She unfolded it, and I saw the surprise then weakening under her poker table eyes.

Oh God, I thought, no El, Liz's got a plan, don't give in. On the other hand, do, we could get out of here in one piece and split it three ways. . .

"Hm," Eleanor sucked her teeth, "I suspect you are aware

that the circumstances of my private life render this an attractive offer. However," she splayed her hands on the table, "I would consider myself negligent if I didn't enquire about the likely consequences of deferring a positive decision at the present moment."

"Well," the boss was momentarily distracted by Liz deciding to stretch out so that she was half lying on her chair, her head leaning back and her eyes closed. I rolled yet another cigarette and started playing with my hair. He coughed, "If you were able to pursue your present course of action, there's no doubt you would be working against the interests of the community here. Business confidence is a fragile thing, especially affected by rumours of time-consuming bureacratic investigations, and if we felt it was best to relocate our operations from Kirktown, it would be a devastating blow to the hard-working people in this area. I don't want to see this happen. And so," he stopped flannelling, "another solution occurs to me. We are on the shores of a beautiful but treacherous bay. It would be regrettable if, after your hours of deviant pleasure, the three of you decided to drive to the shore and go for a walk. There are a lot of quicksands and the tide is treacherous." He looked at Eleanor as if she was a worm, "We can do it, and we will."

"Ah." Eleanor unfolded the paper again, appeared to do some mental calculation and smiled, "Well, gentlemen, I think you can take your offer, stick it and swivel on it."

The room went quiet as a snowfall. For a second, the two corporate men forgot to be menacing, and lost control of their jaw muscles.

"Way to go, El," Liz's sighing voice broke the silence.

"So." Eleanor pushed back her chair, "This meeting which didn't take place is over. We're going. Realistically, you can't stop us without getting into far more trouble than you're in already."

Jock shifted like a hound waiting to be loosed on a hare. The boss leaned forward and gripped Eleanor's wrist. I thought I could smell my fear.

"I don't think you get it," the boss said, "we're not going to let you go. Who do you think you are? Do you think anyone who is anyone cares about you? A small time solicitor

and a couple of other low lifes barely on the margins of society. McSheady, call your men, let's get this thing done."
I clamped my hand over my mouth, unable to stifle my brief wail. I had forgotten Eleanor's advice, and if I thought I had known terror before, I was mistaken.

Jock lifted his mobile, and, like a salmon leaping upstream, Liz rippled into movement. Her hand seemed to caress her nearly full coffee cup before she flung it with shocking force at Jock's face. He dropped his phone, and put his hands up to his nose. Muddy fallout spattered everywhere. There was a muscular scuffle, and a dreadful choked off cry came from the corporate man on my left. I rubbed my eyes. Liz was behind his chair, twisting his right arm up in the same lock the driver and Carl had used on us both. With her other hand, she was holding a knife to his throat. It was her favourite small kitchen knife, which she sometimes brought away with her to cut up fruit in the car. I knew how sharp it was, I had gashed myself on it several times despite her exasperated warnings. When he felt the blade, the man stopped trying to pull her hand away with his left arm and held his breath. The boss made a move towards them both, and Liz nicked her captive's neck, producing a miniature red tide. The sulky teenager had disappeared, and here was a savage container of simmering rage, someone I had never quite seen before.

"Try it," she said, in the voice she had used to Carl at the Bradley site, "try it."

"Liz," Eleanor held out her hand, "they're only bluffing. Don't do. . ."

"Call the police," Liz commanded, giving corporate man's arm another twist, "take Jock's phone and call the police."

Jock put his foot on his phone as it lay on the carpet, "You're no' going to do that, Liz, are you?" he said thickly, blood oozing from his nose.

"Lay a finger on Kate and I will," she said, her eyes forcing him to blink.

"The police won't believe you," the boss said evenly, "three hysterical women breaking in on a meeting and assaulting us . . ."

"Fuck off," Liz replied. I felt the tremor under her voice. My mind switched off. I pulled my sleeve end over my hand, stood up a lot less agilely than Liz, and picked up the empty glass water bottle I had noticed underneath the coffee table. Turning my head, I smashed it against the table edge, and stood, my jagged weapon close to my chest.

"OK," I said madly, "come and drown me, you arseholes."

"Jesus Christ." It was the forgotten driver, his face ashen, "This has gone far enough. I'm going to call the police myself."

He was just about to press the number on his own phone, when a horrendous cacophany of sound reached our ears. An agonised male shriek was followed by a collection of growls, piercing war cries and shouts, and excited barking, and the thunderous pounding of feet rose to a crescendo as the door was flung wide open on its hinges. Carl flew into the room, closely pursued by Oscar straining at a leash in Big Bertha's hands, and a stream of the last people on earth I'd expected to see. It was like one of those dreams where you end up eating cheese with the pope in a hot air balloon, and it all seems perfectly logical. I saw Mighty Martha and Jeanie swinging baseball bats, Alison waving a bicycle chain, Tam bouncing like a dog on speed, Issy, Jack, the stringer from the Grand and Ben, weighed down with a paparazzi-style camera with which he started taking pictures, the flashes exploding like gunfire.

"Hello girls," Issy said, moving rapidly to Eleanor's side, "is this a private party, or can anyone join in?"

17

Grasping that I probably wouldn't need it now, I dropped my broken bottle on to the coffee table, and held on to the back of a chair for support. Beside me, Liz had released her prisoner, and he held his hand to his neck, moaning softly. Through glazed eyes, I watched the stringer and Ben barge past Eleanor and Issy, who were welded together like a sculpture, and push themselves in front of the bossman.

"Can you tell us what's going on here?" the stringer shouted, producing a notebook and a cassette recorder, which he switched on and thrust under the boss's nose. Ben seemed to be taking a close-up of Jock, who had covered his face again, and I could see Oscar still trying to get at Carl for some breakfast. Through the chaos, I saw Jeanie beaming at me, a beacon of insouciant sanity.

"How. . .?" I started. Then Liz shoved by me, her hand to her mouth, and as if attached to her by a twanging cable, I blundered after her into the loo. I held her head while she heaved over the bowl, and she didn't knock me away, nor did she protest at my arms round her waist as she splashed her face at the sink.

"What?" I said to her locked shoulders, seeing her blanched knuckles gripping at the basin, "What is it?"

The racket next door might as well have been coming from an over-loud television. She gulped at the air, as though she had been held under water, her rib-cage straining at her skin, until at last one of her hands left the sink and seized mine.

"I saw the blood," she sounded fit to scream, "I saw it. I would have killed him. What kind of person am I?"

"Jesus." I prised her away from the sink and forced her into my arms. It was like holding a bony tornado. "You wouldn't," I said, suddenly calm, "you wouldn't. Maybe if they'd really attacked us, but you wouldn't otherwise. You saved us, even before this lot arrived. The driver would have called the police, and we'd be ok. You wouldn't, you wouldn't," I repeated, and her breathing steadied a fraction.

"I frighten myself," she said against my neck, "I was so

angry I couldn't stop them putting you into the van, I wanted to kill him. Maybe I'm a psychopath, maybe I'm a really violent, screwed-up. . ."

"OK," I pulled away, put my hands on either side of her face and made her look at me, "You've got an awful temper. I've never had such dreadful fights with anyone as I've had with you. But you've never hit me. It's me who ends up throwing things. If you really were violent and screwed-up, you'd have hurt me loads of times. This was different. And anyway, pyschopaths don't feel what they're doing is wrong, they don't end up barfing at a drop of blood. You're normal, just a bit crosser than most people sometimes. And braver and cleverer and more beautiful," I added, seeing her eyes lose their delirious abstraction. Seeking out our everyday selves, we held each other for a while longer.

"All right," she said finally, her voice not quite normal yet but getting there, "let's face the world."

The room wasn't much quieter. Martha and Bertha were standing by the door, with Oscar casting covetous looks at Carl who was huddled on the floor, while Ben and the stringer, backed up by Jack and Tam, were still badgering Jock and the executives. "What about Mabel, you lackey, what about Mabel?" I heard Jack yell. The bewildered van driver was scratching his head and Eleanor, her face wreathed in smiles, was chattering away to Issy, Jeanie and Alison (who was trying to wipe bicycle chain oil off her hands). Eleanor saw us, and put her thumbs up.

"Nice work, you two," she laughed.

Maybe slightly more convinced that she wasn't going to be branded a menace to society, Liz loosened the grip on my hand which had threatened to do as much harm to my tendons as Carl's knife.

"Well, it's lovely to see you," she said, sounding more like her old self and looking at Issy, "how did you know we were here? How did you. . .?"

"I saw you!" Issy was practically jumping up and down with elation, "I woke up early, and Tam and I were walking in the grounds here. I saw you and El looking like shit in the back of that car and we dived in the shrubbery. Then I saw the van come in as well, and we sneaked up to the stable yard. I heard a man shouting, and knew it was all wrong, so . . ."

"She phoned me!" Jeanie was imitating Tam as well, "And I called the girls, and Issy called Jack who rang that reporter and Ben, and we all met up outside the gates, and then we just charged up the drive and in through the door. It was brilliant, it was like playing cowboys and Indians but better, and we chased that wanker on the door who tried to stop us up to here, and found you. . ." She faltered. The image of Liz holding a knife to someone's throat was clearly reminding her of something she'd rather forget.

"You're a doll," Liz moved forward and gave her a smacking kiss, "I knew you were worth cultivating."

"All right." Eleanor rapped on the table with a cup to call the room to order, and stood like a teacher approaching the end of her tether with a rowdy class, "This is what's going to happen." I think she'd remembered Jock's phrase, and couldn't resist giving him an infinitesimal sneer, "We're definitely going to leave now. We're going to go to my office, have a meeting with my partners and they will take witness statements from me, Kate and Liz, on what happened to us this morning. They'll also take statements from my friends here," she waved her hand around, "and put any photographs with them. The statements will be copied and deposited with various solicitors and other interested bodies. I will continue to work for BAG, and will proceed as I see fit with the information I have so far." She glanced at the pile of computer disks, "You can keep those, they're copies of course." She gave her little sneer again, "I don't think I need to spell this out. Since it's basically our word against yours, the police and the CPS might take the view that there is insufficient evidence for a prosecution against you for assault and kidnap, even if you," she gave the van driver a brief smile, "were willing to testify for us. However, I won't be able to prevent rumours of what happened here spreading around, or stop this reporter from writing what he wants, and you'd have to be even more stupid than I think you are to wish any little accidents on us." She drew herself up, and for the first time, I saw how furiously angry she was, "We may not be anyone who is anyone," she said, passion breaking into her voice, "but we can be fucking noisy, and we won't be treated like this again."

I wanted to cheer, and Jack did. I looked at the boss,

whose face was impassive, and at his side-kicks. They were both dwindling in their seats, and behind their clean-shaven masks, I saw the spectres of investigations, loss of bonuses, downsizing and unemployment flitting.

"Och well," Jock's nose had dried up and his voice was clearer, "that's me. I'm for my bed." He sighed and looked at a bloody handkerchief, "Ambrose Dexter the Third, consider my contract with you ended. There'll be a clause somewhere allowing it, nae doubt. I'll send you a bill, and add a bit on if I need surgery. We'll be off the site tomorrow. Rock tours, that's the business to get into. Mud-wrestling with hippies and dealing with mad lesbians is no' my idea of fun." He looked at me without animosity, "Pity you're no' better connected in the music world. Still, if you make it big and want some security. . ."

It struck me that he could give Liz a run for her money in the amorality stakes.

"Just a minute," Liz stood in front of him as he made a move for the door, "you owe me."

"Oh aye." He pulled a roll of notes from his trouser pocket, "You're no' going to believe this, but there was a genuine hold up that morning. I must have just missed you."

"Yeah?" Liz was unimpressed, "So how come you weren't arrested in that bust?"

"Ah," he started tapping his nose, then thought the better of it, "you heard about that. A little bird suggested that it was a line I should move out of for the time being. Here." He handed over a wad of notes and a handful of coins.

"This is short," Liz said in disbelief.

"Come on, I've had to make a wee deduction for that crate of beer. Business is business." His eyes challenged hers.

"You're a crook and a vicious bastard," Liz's jaw was set, "what if I go to the police?"

"Go ahead. I doubt they'll be interested by now. There's enough other people in the trade to keep them busy. Mind you," he gave her what probably passed for a frank look with him, "I doubt I'll be working in this area in the near future. You're obviously no' my favourite person at the moment," he touched his nose more gingerly this time, "but I'm no' one for going round settling personal scores when it's more bother than it's worth." There was neither anger nor apology in his tone, and I was conscious of a deal being struck.

Liz looked at the money for a while, began to stuff it into her pocket and then pulled it out again and put it on the table in front of Eleanor. "For the fighting fund, if you'll take it," she muttered.

Eleanor pursed her lips. I gazed at the cash. There must have been over a hundred quid there. Spare change to the executives, a good part of my rent or lots of food and tobacco to me, a ream of photocopying to BAG, more than his weekly pension to Jack. . . Eleanor pushed the money over to Liz's victim.

"Buy yourself a new shirt," she said coldly, "you've got blood on that one."

The room was quiet again. Jock snorted, "Come on boys, we're finished here, expect Jed's still hanging round at the back door, missing all the excitement." He glanced at Carl, "Didn't know you were scared of dogs."

Carl gave him an agonised look, and began to run at a crouch out of the room, only to be blocked by Liz. Trapped between her and Oscar's jaws glooping dribble on to the back of his legs, I observed him trying to make himself tiny.

"Just remember," Liz's voice was like a still, bottomless millpond, "if I see you again, I'll get this dog to chew your balls off."

She withdrew, and let him flee. Jock and the van driver followed more slowly, and Eleanor pressed a card into the driver's hand.

"If you ever need a solicitor," I heard her say, "free consultation and all that." He couldn't smile, but took the card anyway, and after their carpet-deadened footsteps had receded, we all made a general beeline for the door.

"You can't stay on your guard forever, Miss Knighton," Dexter was giving us his parting shot, "there are far more. . . effective people around than McSheady."

"And you can't stay outside the law forever," Eleanor removed her hand from Issy's back to face him, the table length between them.

"You're very naive, for a member of the legal profession. You should know the big guys always win."

"Maybe, Mr Dexter," Eleanor flicked the folded paper with his price on across the polished surface, "although it's fun to fight. Carry on talking, you're back on tape."

The stringer smiled, "Mr Dexter, would you care to elaborate on what you've just said?"

He obviously didn't, and we walked towards the door. The strain and exhaustion began to exact their toll. Somehow my shoes had been replaced by lead lined diving boots, and my body was a stringless puppet.

"Thanks," I offered to Bertha as we met in the doorway, "thanks, really." I'd never spoken to her before.

"That's all right," she said in an amazingly sweet high-pitched voice, "Martha and me'll be able to have a little browse in Kirktown, won't we dear? Come on, lovely boy," she fondled Oscar's ears, "let's get you a nice bone for being so good."

I should feel overjoyed at being rescued, I thought, wading through the thick carpet of the passage and trying not to fall headlong down a wide staircase to the airy front hall below, and I don't. I want to find my violin and go to sleep. The bright fresh daylight dazzled me, and I clung on to Liz's arm while we congregated outside the front door. I barely registered the sight of the car and van disappearing out of the gates, or of Jack picking himself a bouquet of flowers from a border. I did see that Eleanor and Issy were gazing at each other like women with only one thing on their minds, until Issy lifted her wrist to see her watch.

"It's nine o'clock. The shop," she said, consternation spreading over her features.

"Don't be daft." Jeanie was still bouncing, "Me and Alison'll mind it. Give us the keys and we'll be off. We won't bankrupt you."

Arranging phrases whirled around me. "My violin, my violin," I was saying, "where's the car, I must find it."

"OK, Kate." Liz was holding me, "We think the car'll be on River Quay. Ben and Mark are going to drive us back. El's staying here, she'll pick her stuff up from us later."

"The statements," another random concern popped like a pin ball against my forehead, "we've got to make statements."

"Next week, sweetie, come on."

I tried to thank everyone again, although they were being irritating by refusing to stay in focus, walked down a drive which was behaving like the deck of a cross Channel ferry, and passed out in the back of a car, which must have belonged to Mark, the stringer, because when I came to, he was driving us through the city.

"Oh," I unstuck my tongue from the roof of my mouth, "we're here."

"She's alive!" Ben turned round to me, "We were going to drop you off at the morgue."

"Don't," Liz was a bit snappy, "not after this morning."

"What are we going to do if we can't find the car?" I wasn't sure if I felt all right or on the verge of a nervous breakdown.

"Go to the police," Liz said. This reliance on the law was something I'd never expected from her, let alone twice in one day, and I put my head back on her shoulder.

Mark crawled along the uneven surface of River Quay. All the cars parked in front of the seedy hotels looked like the kind that are soldered together from at least two accident write-offs, so the Fiesta didn't seem too out of place, squeezed in between an ancient jaguar and a skip. Life had returned in the form of needles of anxiety jabbing me all over, and I fought my way out of the car to grope under the wheel arches for the keys. They fell to the mucky tarmac; I scratched them up with stiff fingers and opened the boot. There was my violin, nestling among our bags, and not a scrap of rubbish in the rest of the jumbled interior had been moved an inch out of place. I hugged my instrument like a long lost child.

"I'll sort the wedding out." Ben said to Liz, "Get some rest, and we'll talk tomorrow. Sure you're ok now, you don't want to come back to mine for something to eat and to chat?"

We shook our heads. It was another horrible sensation to get into our car which some malevolent stranger had casually driven here, and we both wound down our windows.

"I'll be in touch soon." Mark cut through our stunted efforts to express undying gratitude, "To get your stories straight and stuff. Drive carefully."

That was the thing. Liz's hands quivered on the wheel, and the effort of starting the engine and getting us moving pushed beads of sweat on to her forehead.

"Shall I drive?" I asked, my arms clamped round my violin.

"No. I can do it."

She bumped and crept through the Saturday morning traffic which came at us from all the wrong angles. Were we at home, or had we been dumped in some foreign metropolis where everyone drove on the other side of the road? I was only convinced when I had carried my case into our front room, and risked leaving it while I helped Liz fetch armfuls of bags inside. Now all I had to do was organise myself to be at the arts centre at one. . .

"Kate," Liz stopped me unpacking bags on the floor to look for a clean shirt I knew I had in there somewhere, "I'm going to phone Fred and Jo. I don't think you can play today."

"But I must," I was practically weeping with frustration, "if I can just find that shirt, I'll be fine."

"Oh darling," I realised that her lips were grey, "I think we're in a bit of a state. I'm phoning."

She said things like "a little accident" and "ok, but shaken up" down the line. We drank some tea, had a bath and tried to go to bed.

It was almost as terrifying as being held in Bolton House. We took it in turns to wake up crying and shouting at the formless shadows jumping out from the bedroom walls, one or other of us trapped in a sticky layer between the cheerful day outside and the ordinary oblivion of repose. Countless times, Liz assured me that Dexter and his executives would not dare to try and harm us again, not now that they could be exposed, and that Carl wasn't in the room with a gang of his mates, and just as often I told her she wasn't a murderess, and that her hands were clean. We ferried endless cups of tea up the stairs, we got up and went to the corner shop for stacks of chocolate then scuttled back, paranoid when we were on our own and unable to face talking to anyone else. We felt safest in bed, yet there the dreams would start, and we considered venturing out again to score some tranquilisers. It must have been after midnight when I finally woke up and sensed that I wasn't going to call a doctor and beg for us both to be committed. I felt hungry, the walls were in their proper places, and Liz's regular breathing told me she was at peace. I lay for a while, half querying whether I could be bothered to get up and make a sandwich, and half thinking deep thoughts on how easy it was to slide into a place where you wanted to harm someone. How odd, I thought, that Liz's gentle skin, getting so familiar under my hand, enclosed such a mass of contradictions. Her easy self-reliance, her terrible anger, her tenderness to me, her wonderful desire. . . My lips were in the soft pleat between her neck and shoulder, and there was something I wanted to do probably more than make a sandwich.

"Wha'?" She was waking up, "What are you. . .?"

"Guess," I said through the quilt, wriggling down to put my mouth to her shapely foot, "but I'll stop at your knees if you insist."

"Nice?" I enquired somewhat superfluously when she'd quietened down. She replied deliciously in kind, and I held out until our bodies had stilled and we had indulged in a heap of billing and cooing before going in for the kill.

"Li-iz, light of my life and best-lover-I've-ever-had, I'm so hungry."

"Great." She squeezed me with her legs, "You mean to say this was all just to get me to cook you something in the middle of the night?"

"Of course. You know my priorities." Although the feel of her against me again made me ponder whether I really was quite so peckish.

She flung the quilt aside, "All right, come and peel some potatoes, and I'll make you the best chips you've ever had."

We sat up against the pillows, sharing a great bowl along with a heart attack of salt and a bloodbath of ketchup.

"You know, Kate," I could see the cogs turning in her head, "it's like what Issy told us ages ago about the Great Raid."

"You what?" She was right, these were definitely the best chips I'd ever eaten.

"Like, the ordinary people got done over, and no-one protected them, even those that were meant to. It's the same now. Everyone depends on these big businesses, and they don't give a shit as long as they make money. We're all expendable, and end up being nasty to each other. What a world."

I smiled fondly at her disgruntled frown, "You're quite a closet intellectual, aren't you? As well as being a fantastic cook."

"Piss off, you're not as stupid as you make out either. Though I think you'd have died from beri-beri or rickets if I hadn't caught you in time."

"So how come you're such a good cook anyway?" I asked after we'd had a ketchup flavoured kiss.

"Er," she gave a secretive smile, "Derek, my step-father, actually."

"Oh?" She'd hardly told me anything about him.

"Yeah. My mother's a dreadful cook. Almost in your class. And when he came along, I knew I had to hate him on principle; I gave him hell most of the time. But I used to sit in the kitchen, pretending I was reading my comics, and really I was watching him. Trying to see what he was doing to make stuff that tasted so nice. And now," I wasn't used to her being so forthcoming about herself, "that's what we do together if I ever visit. We cook, and he tells me not to upset ma, and I tell him I'm good for her because he and the others are too nice to her and I keep her mentally alert and did you mean what you said about me being the best lover you'd ever had?"

"What?" I'd been holding my breath in case she clammed up, "Of course, you must know that by now." Surely I'd told her this a hundred times.

"Ah," she gave me her under the eyebrows look, "can I tell you something?"

"Yes," I murmured drippily, almost expecting the compliment I'd never dared hope for.

"You're a beautiful woman, and I'd do anything for you," she prodded my nose with a chip, "but that's the last time I give that Eleanor a lift anywhere ever again."

18

The heebie-jeebies didn't quite end there. The worst nightmares stopped, but I think we were both aware over the next few weeks of some shapeless threat hanging round the edges of our lives, restricting our normal movements. As insurance, each of us told practically everyone we knew what had happened, and an aghast band started making sure, not so subtly, that I was never left to make my own way home after gigs in the city, or even to step unaccompanied from the van to our front door. It was obvious to me that Liz was also employing all sorts of subterfuges to avoid walking alone at night or leaving me on my own in the house for any length of time. Luckily, on the day after our adventure, I didn't realise that Dexter would gain this particular psychological victory, so I thought I was quite recovered when Eleanor and Issy called round late in the afternoon. We had been doing our usual thing, with me sawing through the fast movement of the violin concerto in the front room, and Liz tinkering with her bike in the sunny back yard.

"You know," Liz came back into the house, smears of black up her arms, "I think I'll offer that heap of shit to Jeanie. She can give me what she wants for it, and do it up or sell it for scrap."

"But darling, I thought you loved it. We were going to go for little jaunts. . ." I couldn't quite believe what I'd heard.

"Yer, well," she sounded embarrassed, "I know my mum's never liked me having a bike and er," she transferred black from her forearm to her forehead, "it's not nice, worrying about someone like she must have. . .oh fuck, I've a dreadful feeling I'm approaching something like emotional maturity."

"Oh my." I put my bow and violin down, and let my eyes travel all over her. It was a reaction to shock, what I was feeling, we'd only been up for about two hours. "Come here," I said anyway, "I think I missed a bit of you last time."

It was more luck that we'd finished the most interesting part and were on to discussing childhood pets by the time the knock came at the door and we heard Issy's voice from the street.

"Is this a good idea? They might be. . ." Two separate giggles came through the bedroom window, and I poked my head out to address the close tops of their heads,

"We were. But we can have a tea break. Give us a sec. and I'll come down."

We sat around Liz's dismembered machine in the yard, dissecting the previous day's events in the sun-warmed security of our flaking walls. It wasn't at all odd to see Eleanor and Issy together, leaning against each other and exchanging pregnant looks, it was more like seeing the last two missing pieces of a jigsaw being slotted into place.

"We've just come to pick up the stuff I had in your car, really," Eleanor said, "I guessed you'd have phoned if you hadn't found it. Where was it?"

"On River Quay." I arranged shreds of tobacco in a paper, "They must have driven it there to set us up for our little orgy." Liz's shoulder tensed against mine.

"El," she disguised her mouth with her mug, "do you think they really were bluffing? Was it awful what I did with the knife and all?" She'd told me she'd realised the knife was in her pocket all along, but had been too frightened about what was happening to me in the van to produce it earlier.

Eleanor looked firmly at her, "I don't honestly know. I suppose my instinct tells me they were, but we couldn't know that for sure, and besides, we didn't know Issy and the cavalry were going to arrive. It could have been a lot more unpleasant for us if you hadn't done your stuff." She saw Liz's eyes sliding away, "Don't beat yourself up about it, we know you don't make a habit of sticking knives into people."

There was a short, not entirely comfortable, pause.

"So, what happens next?" I asked to break the silence.

"Well," Eleanor was pink to her hairline, "we're actually on our way to Toni's for me to fetch some things. I'm going to commute from Issy's for a while, until we. . ."

"Wear yourselves out?" I suggested, and laughed impolitely, "I really meant about Boltons and Bradleys, I wasn't trying to nose into your private life. Are we going to make statements? Was that Dexter man the big chief? What does it all mean?"

"Oh Lord, all this hasn't been exactly uppermost in my mind." Eleanor absentmindedly pulled a leaf from a mint plant in my neglected old sink of herbs and rubbed it between her fingers, "Yeah, I think it would be a good idea if you came along to the office some time next week, and we could get it all down. I'm going to pass on the disks like I said. I mean, they must have been up to something really naughty for them to be so heavy-handed. Time will tell, I guess."

I looked at her more closely when Liz and Issy had disappeared inside to fetch more tea and some cake.

"OK," she said eventually, "I can tell you're dying to know. I told Amy about me and Issy and she wasn't best pleased. She didn't believe that we haven't, you know, up 'til now, either. It's going to be bloody difficult, sorting out the house and everything. . .still," she smiled in the direction of the open back door, "I think it'll be worth it." She kicked my foot, "As long as we don't go on attracting trouble like you and Liz seem to do."

"We don't. . ." I started, then stopped. She was right. My life had been marvellously uneventful before I met Liz, and now, in less than twelve months, I had been through enough traumas to keep me in therapy for years. Then I heard Liz laugh at something Issy was saying, and felt the imprint of her body still hovering in mine.

"Ah, it's worth it," I said.

"What's worth it?" Liz came back out in the yard, and balanced the cake on the seat of her bike.

"Worth putting up with you for the sake of your baking," I said, putting my arm around her as she settled beside me.

"And I thought it was all the kinky sex you liked. Fruit cake anyone?"

It was all somewhat of an anti-climax after that. I suppose I had expected some kind of dramatic denouement, with our travails splashed across the front pages of the national newspapers, interviews with high-ranking policemen, and top-level officials descending en masse to wreak revenge on the perfidious management of Dexter Holdings. Instead, we dictated statements to an impassive secretary at Eleanor's office, and then carried on uneasily, as if waiting for some inevitable retribution to fall. Eleanor wouldn't even tell us how much Dexter had offered her as a bribe, Liz heard through Ben that the papers had rejected Mark's stories as libellous, and I found myself seriously weighing up the pros and cons of investing in a dog like Oscar. Then one morning, a little early for me, I was wandering around the city centre on a sort of mission for the band to check out the price of air fares to the States, so we could compare them with what was on offer on the internet, and continue our debate over pre-booked security versus last minute rock bottom bargains. Liz was working all day, and I was busy telling myself that it wasn't dread at being on my own in the empty house that had driven me out, when I came out of one travel agents and thought I saw Jock walking towards me. I think I gave a little shriek, and I certainly fled. I didn't care what other pedestrians thought of me as I barged my way down the street, puffed through an alley, dived into a department store and sped hysterically up an escalator.

Trembling and shaking, I slunk like a pervert to the far corner of Lingerie, where I mopped my face and wondered where the ladies loos were. If I hadn't lost him by now, surely he wouldn't follow me there. I could stay until closing time, when I would ask the staff to ring Liz to come and fetch me. Or I could shoplift one of those black lacy nightdresses and get arrested. I'd be safe in a cell. . . After about five minutes of this, I came at least partially to my senses, and realised that if it had been Jock, he hadn't followed me. I pretended to look at socks until my heart and limbs had recovered from the shock and exercise, and my mind had switched to considering self-defence classes. I would go to a cafe where they allowed smoking, and think about this some more. I couldn't live the rest of my life in this state of low level fear interspersed with moments of blind terror, it would drive me properly barmy in no time. Fired with resolution, I left the store at a normal pace, and strode with confidence into one of my favourite haunts.

Walking back from the counter with my tray and heading for a free table, I came face to face with the purposeful and rather pissed off visage of the van driver.

"Shit," I thought, stopping myself from dropping everything on the floor, "is this a conspiracy to make me die of fright?"

"Saw you come in here," he grunted, "want a word with you."

I knew my legs weren't up to another bout of sprinting, and I sat heavily down.

He joined me and put the local newspaper in front of me, "Seen this yet, have you?"

I instructed my eyes to focus, and looked at the headline, "Bradley site for sale." Heart jolting once more, I scanned the article, horribly aware of his disapproving breathing opposite me. Among the verbiage, all it said was that the Bradley consortium, having run into financial difficulties, had put the site, complete with planning permission, on the market. It ended with a council official's platitude that he expected buyers to quickly form an orderly queue for the chance of purchasing this unique business opportunity. There was no mention of Boltons or of Dexter Holdings. I put the paper down, and dared to look into the driver's eyes.

"Looks like you won," he said, "McSheady's going abroad, I lost my job, and I hear Boltons are going to be investigated for financial jiggery pokery, which'll probably mean they close as well. Bet nothing's changed in your life."

A flash of temper saved me. "Don't blame me," I snapped, "your lot aren't the ones still having nightmares. Anyway, the management at Bradleys and Boltons know the law. No-one told them to break it like they did with their dodgy accounting." Eleanor's disks must have finally come good.

"That yank Dexter did," he said, pulling out a cigarette, "Dexter Holdings is a family concern. He's one of the sons."

"What?"

"Yeah," he lit up, "McSheady told me the story. As he understood it, Dexter Holdings were fed up with bankrolling Bradleys through the planning stages and set-up time. Dexter told Bradleys and Boltons to sort it out themselves. Then he came over when it looked like your solicitor friend was going to cause trouble, a day or two before the shit hit the fan." He saw all the questions in my eyes, "We'd been keeping an eye on her for weeks. When she didn't turn up at her office that Friday morning, McSheady called her firm and found out she'd gone to Scotland. He told the management who put two and two together, spoke to Jess and told McSheady to grab you all when you turned up."

"Would you have killed us?" I couldn't believe I'd just said that in this homely cafe.

172

He scoffed. "Not me. I reckon they only wanted to scare you off. I'd have called the police, though, if your mates hadn't arrived." His expression changed to a mixture of contempt and shame, "It's a rough world out there. Best stick to your own kind and what you know."

"Maybe." Now I wasn't even sure myself if we'd done the right thing. We'd scared ourselves silly, and probably helped Eleanor to wreck Kirktown's economy. Our triumphant rescue from the evil clutches of big business by a handful of friends and dogs was getting lost in a morass of doubt. Would the Bradley development have been such a bad thing anyway? Would something worse be constructed in its place? In the last few weeks, the protest camp had shrunk, and would anyone have the inclination or energy to start up again if the site was sold to another bunch of developers? The only consolation I could think of as the van driver left was that we couldn't be in any danger from Dexter Holdings any more, not if the law had caught up with Boltons' creative accounting. I drank my tea and tried to feel happy and relaxed.

Life went on, and on a July afternoon, I returned to the house from playing at a weekend festival. I was hot, tired and dispirited, and Liz was nowhere to be seen. She had worked out her partnership deal with Ben, with the proviso that she would be away with us for six months in the following year, and had thrown herself into the business. She hadn't come down to pick me up, like she might have done previously, and had sounded tense and offhand on the phone the day before. I showered and put on cleaner clothes, letting myself consider the possibility that she had changed her mind about going to the States, and exploring the extent to which, at this precise moment, I actually cared. The door banged and she came in, her expression full of reserve.

"Good, you're back. Come on." She picked up my excuse for a handbag and a pair of my sneakers, "Got your fags?"

"What?" My mouth opening and shutting, I let her pull me out of the house and into the car, "Where. . .?"

"Wait and see," she muttered, and drove in silence to the city outskirts, ignoring my increasingly cross questions. I was about to yell at her to stop the car and let me out so I could escape her taciturn stonewalling, when she turned up the drive of a country house hotel, the kind of place I'd never stayed in since I'd left Chloe and her regular salary.

"Here we are," she said, the corners of her mouth escaping from her attempt to keep it rigid, "get out then."

I followed her striding legs over warm flags, into a cool scented hall and up a baronial staircase. She fished a key from her back pocket and opened a door, "Well?"

If I hadn't known her better, I would have said she was nervous. I stepped into the peaceful cream room, and took in the huge bed, the massive bunch of flowers on a side table and the open bathroom door revealing what looked suspiciously like a jacuzzi. Nothing sensible came out of my mouth, and I saw the hesitancy in her eyes.

She put her hands on my shoulders, "Kate, I knew you'd forget. It's a year since we first met. I'm breaking all my records here, help me out."

We studied each other's faces for a long time, until she moved to put the "Do Not Disturb" on the door and to lock it behind her. The bed felt fit for royalty, and I couldn't detect even the slightest squeak.

"Oh dear," I said after a while as I undid her jeans, enjoying the way she drew in her breath and the look of absorption settling on her features, "we didn't bring any luggage."

"Ah babe," she lifted her hips so I could ease the garments off, "I was kind of hoping we wouldn't need any. I could only afford one night."